# LOVE
## is the
# ONLY STORY

By Ben Schrank

*Consent*
*Miracle Man*

# LOVE
is the
# ONLY STORY

## tales of romance

edited by Ben Schrank

## THE LYONS PRESS

Guilford, Connecticut
An Imprint of The Globe Pequot Press

The Lyons Press is an imprint of
The Globe Pequot Press.

First Lyons Press edition, January 2003

Printed in the United States of America
Text design by Claire Zoghb

Library of Congress Cataloging-in-Publication Data

Davis, Lydia.
  [My husband and I]
  Love is the only story : tales of romance / edited by Ben Schrank.--
1st Lyons Press ed.
      p. cm.
  ISBN 1-58574-748-3 (hc : alk. paper)
  I. Schrank, Ben. II. Kawabata, Yasunari, 1899-1972. Frightening love.
III. Title: Frightening love. IV. Title.
  PS3554.A9356 M9 2003
  813'.54--dc21

                          2002153391

For MBB

# Contents

Ben Schrank   ix
Introduction

Lydia Davis   1
My Husband and I

Anton Chekhov   3
The Lady with the Dog

Leonard Michaels   31
Of Mystery There Is No End

Isaac Babel   57
The Kiss

Dagoberto Gilb   67
Maria de Covina

Djuna Barnes   83
Behind the Heart

Italo Calvino   93
The Memoirs of Casanova

Michelle Cliff  107
Art History

William Trevor  123
Mr. Tennyson

Rikki Ducornet  141
The Student from Algiers

Charles Bukowski  159
The Most Beautiful Woman in Town

John Edgar Wideman  169
Doc's Story

Anzia Yezierska  183
Hunger

George Saunders  205
The Barber's Unhappiness

Yasunari Kawabata  245
Frightening Love

Acknowledgments  247

# Introduction

## Ben Schrank

The best love stories aren't about falling in love. Instead, they are about the times just before, or after, or better still they grapple with the obstacles we create in order to block a chance at love. These are the moments that we readers know well. We long to get close to the hidden moment of falling, but not so close that it blinds us. Often we're suddenly looking behind us for it. Did we just pass it? Was it as perfect as we'd hoped? The stories in this anthology take our understanding of love and send it sprawling. They make us reconsider the time that surrounds love. They give no answers and provide few clues. The best don't even bother with admonishments.

Great love stories bring the confusion of real life to tropes that we understand all too well. In "The Most

Beautiful Woman in Town," Charles Bukowski gives us Cass, the prostitute who destroys her beauty and won't stop until she is gone. The Bukowski story was in a collection that a poet friend of my mother's gave me when I was twelve. I read it through several times in my room and found that I could no longer think clearly and so I refused to come down to dinner. Could beauty really destroy someone? I hadn't known. Cass has stuck with me since, though I won't say I love everything Bukowski wrote. But in Cass, he showed us longing. It's an almost shameful feeling, missing Cass. Loving her is indulgent, excessively romantic, but it is not wrong. Instead, it is lonely. Bukowski writes, "The night kept coming on in and there was nothing I could do."

I believe in Cass as strongly as I believe in Anzia Yezierska's immigrant girl, Shenah Pessah, who says, "Can I help it what's in my heart? It always longs in me for the higher." Her love is honest and unfettered by the weak ploy of irony. I found Yezierska's story at the back of the Brooklyn Public Library while looking for a friend's novel, and I read it standing up, slowly overheating in my wool overcoat, waves of warmth rushing to my temples. But I was unable to move at all till I'd finished reading. I completely embraced the idea of Shenah Pessah's heart bursting with unrequited love. Her willingness to equate love with doing better feels charming, real; a true volition for a young immigrant woman, because it will forever defy resolution. Like any true romantic, Shenah Pessah is in love with the idea of stumbling forever after a dream.

The men and women in these stories know that they can count on being alone. Their few moments of solace, of actually being in love, will be fleeting. Italo Calvino's Casanova seems baffled by the realization that the part he plays in the lives of his loves is a small one. He is bitter and honest with himself when he realizes that for all his efforts, his Fulvia has only discovered herself, while he fell in love with her. But who can know this better than our Casanovas? They are like soul mechanics, like teachers, like William Trevor's Mr. Tennyson, who calls out to Chinny Martin's beloved Jenny to stay after class so that he may tell her about his own broken heart. Poor Mr. Tennyson becomes a signpost, a warning to all those who know him, to beware the bad things that come with impossible loves.

But we readers don't listen to shrill warnings. We've all ridden a bicycle back and forth on the cobbled street in front of a lover's house, hoping to see a shadow, either at the window or through the front door. Hours pass and it's time to return home, but leaving is inconceivable. It doesn't matter that we're terribly conspicuous and that without speaking of our feelings, our love will never be returned. This may not be romantic, but it's a real love, dense with longing. It would be terribly wrong to tell Chinny that he doesn't have a true love for Jenny. Trevor doesn't presume so much. He may call Chinny's love silly, and it is only incidental to the grander sadness in Mr. Tennyson. But that makes it no less real to Chinny.

Love and longing are the divining rods of modern fiction. Without them, nothing worth looking for can ever be found. Writers know that readers understand what it is to long for another person. This longing is more than the underlying motif for love stories. It becomes central to the covenant writers make with us. So long as they do not resolve the idea, we will come round to hear the story again. There is an endearing endlessness to the need to tell and to hear the stories constructed around love. Writers are assured that no matter how esoteric their description of love, its universality will allow any reader entrance. How can our brains have developed this stunning set of problems and questions and events, that seem never to allow us the questionable pleasure (even here I cannot grapple with the combination of pleasure and resolution without putting a question before it) of resolution? This human feeling of longing is an ugly kind of luck, as arbitrary and inexplicable as any evolutionary oddity, like goose bumps, or the need for leadership. Longing is also a wonderfully pervasive human sensation. Once we look for it, it can be found not just in stories of romance, but in every story.

Djuna Barnes helps us to expand our idea of how many kinds of love might be romantic. The love she writes about exists between a young boy and an older woman who is about to die, and it is certainly as filled with longing as the tragically conventional loss that Rikki Ducornet explores in "The Student from Algiers." There is death in Michelle Cliff's "Art History," which is suffused with the hauntings of love. Kawabata's "Frightening Love" is also about death, but it is the longing that drives it, even in its brevity. Leonard Michaels's "Of Mystery There is No End" is metaphysical in his approach to longing. A mathematician wonders at love, at its qualities and his own involvement with it, against the backdrop of his own loneliness. And then there's Isaac Babel, who writes of love as a strange aside, a look of frustration on young Elizaveta Alekseyevna's part when the narrator leaves for war. It is a moment lost in the rush to battle. "When will you take us from here?" she asks. And there, her drive to survive is more evident, more base and necessary than simple love.

But mostly this collection is filled with stories about longing over errors, missed chances, misunderstandings. There is sweetness too, in the form of George Saunders's "The Barber's Happiness." And there is hope, in John Edgar Wideman's "Doc's Story." I read Wideman's story aloud with a group of eighth graders when I was a young public school teacher in Manhattan, and I was nearly fired the next day. I had foolishly believed that the story's transformational dream trumped its atmosphere. In a longish meeting, the principal and several concerned parents did not agree with me. Perhaps I should have tried to describe what it meant to me to receive Bukowski's stories at that age, how the lifestyle in the fiction didn't matter to me nearly as much as the admission that any dalliance of any kind with love would be wildly frustrating—it wouldn't just be another puzzle that would disappear with the end of adolescence. I might have said, "Can't you see what is inspirational here? Stories like these are what will keep you alive." But the principal didn't encourage me to speak out that day. I find that now, I still give love stories to friends. I send them with notes that say "Try this" or "For your consideration," and I get out of the way.

When I described this collection to friends, they always mentioned Chekhov's "The Lady with the Dog." I read it again and saw that I needed to include it, because it negates my argument; it does seem to capture something that I've said defies containment. I must also add that I've left out other stories like it, that are worthy of many readings, like stories from Raymond Carver's What We Talk About When We Talk About Love, and Harold Brodkey's First Love and Other Sorrows; Alberto Moravia's Roman Tales, and works by Ann Beattie, Alice Munro, Alice Adams, and by thousands of others. You could read forever and read only about love.

What I hope to give you here is a collection of love stories as difficult and rewarding as any great love affair. They are full of odd notions, desperate pleas, and doomed actions. None perfectly expresses what you or I might say when we say love, when we are feeling upright, and good. While we yearn for a more perfect, static kind of love, these stories call out to us. They are patient. They know we will return to them. And they will be there, ready to help us indulge the wonderfully human habits of love and longing.

# LOVE
## is the
# ONLY STORY

# My Husband and I

Lydia Davis

My husband and I are Siamese twins. We are joined at the forehead. Our mother feeds us. When we are moved to copulate we join lower down as well forming a loop like a certain espaliered tree. Time passes. I separate from my husband below and give birth to twins who are not joined together as we are. They squirm on the ground. Our mother cares for them. They are most often asymmetrical with each other, even in sleep when they lie still. Awake, they stay near each other, as though elastic bands held them, and near us and near our mother. At night the bond is even stronger and we snap together and lie in a heap, my husband's hard muscles against my soft muscles, against our mother's stringy old muscles, and our babies' feather muscles, our arms around one another like so many snakes, and distant thumping music in the fields behind us.

# The Lady with the Dog

## Anton Chekhov

1.

People had been telling one another that a newcomer had been seen on the promenade—a lady with a dog. Dmitri Dmtrich Gurov had been a fortnight in Yalta[1], and was accustomed to its ways, and he, too, had begun to take an interest in fresh arrivals. From his seat in Vernet's outdoor café, he caught sight of a young woman in a toque, passing along the promenade; she was fair and not very tall; after her trotted a white Pomeranian.

Later he encountered her in the municipal park and in the square several times a day. She was always alone, wearing the same toque, and the Pomeranian always trotted at her side. Nobody knew who she was, and people simply referred to her as "the lady with the dog."

"If she's here without her husband, and without any friends," thought Gurov, "it wouldn't be a bad idea to make her acquaintance."

He was not yet forty but had a twelve-year-old daughter and two sons in high school. He had been talked into marrying in his third year of college, and his wife now looked nearly twice as old as he did. She was a tall woman with dark eyebrows, erect, dignified, imposing, and, as she said of herself, a "thinker." She was a great reader, omitted the "hard sign"[2] at the end of her words in her letters, and called her husband "Dimitry" instead of Dmitry; and though he secretly considered her shallow, narrow-minded, and dowdy, he stood in awe of her, and disliked being at home. He had first begun deceiving her long ago and he was now constantly unfaithful to her, and this was no doubt why he spoke slightingly of women, to whom he referred as *the lower race.*

He considered that the ample lessons he had received from bitter experience entitled him to call them whatever he liked, but without this "lower race" he could not have existed a single day. He was bored and ill-at-ease in the company of men, with whom he was always cold and reserved, but felt quite at home among women, and knew exactly what to say to them, and how to behave; he could even be silent in their company without feeling the slightest awkwardness. There was an elusive charm in his appearance and disposition which attracted women and caught their sympathies. He knew this and was himself attracted to them by some invisible force.

Repeated and bitter experience had taught him that every fresh intimacy, while at first introducing such pleasant variety into everyday life, and offering itself as a charming, light adventure, inevitably developed, among decent people (especially in Moscow, where they are so irresolute and slow to move), into a problem of excessive complication leading to an intolerably irksome situation. But every time he encountered an attractive woman he forgot all about this experience, the desire for life surged up in him, and everything suddenly seemed simple and amusing.

One evening, then, while he was dining at the restaurant in the park, the lady in the toque came strolling up and took a seat at a neighboring table. Her expression, gait, dress, coiffure, all told him that she was from the upper classes, that she was married, that she was in Yalta for the first time, alone and bored....The accounts of the laxity of morals among visitors to Yalta are greatly exaggerated, and he paid no heed to them, knowing that for the most part they were invented by people who would gladly have transgressed themselves, had they known how to set about it. But when the lady sat down at a neighboring table a few yards from him, these stories of easy conquests, of excursions to the mountains, came back to him, and the seductive idea of a brisk transitory liaison, an affair with a woman whose very name he did not know, suddenly took possession in his mind.

He snapped his fingers at the Pomeranian, and when it trotted up to him, shook his forefinger at it. The Pomeranian growled. Gurov shook his finger again.

The lady glanced at him and instantly lowered her eyes.

"He doesn't bite," she said, and blushed.

"May I give him a bone?" he asked, and on her nod of consent added in friendly tones: "Have you been long in Yalta?"

"About five days."

"And I am dragging out my second week here."

Neither spoke for a few minutes.

"The days pass quickly, and yet one is so bored here," she said, not looking at him.

"It's the thing to say it's boring here. People never complain of boredom in godforsaken holes like Belyev or Zhinzdra, but when they get here it's: 'Oh, the dullness! Oh, the dust!' You'd think they'd come from Granada to say the least."

She laughed. Then they both went on eating in silence, like complete strangers. But after dinner they left the restaurant together, and embarked upon the light, jesting talk of people free and contented, for whom it is all the same where they go, or what they talk about. They strolled along, remarking on the strange light over the sea. The water was a warm, tender purple, the moonlight lay on its surface in a golden strip. They said how close it was, after the hot day. Gurov told her he was from Moscow, had a degree in literature but worked in a bank; that he had at one time trained himself to sing in a private opera company, but had given up the idea; that he owned two houses in Moscow....And from her he learned that she had grown up in Petersburg, but had gotten married in the town of S., where she had been living two years, that she would stay another month in Yalta, and that perhaps her husband, who needed a rest, would join her. She was quite unable to explain whether her husband was a member of the province council, or on the board of the *zemstvo*,[3] and was greatly amused at herself for this. Further, Gurov learned her name was Anna Sergeyevna.

Back in his own room he thought about her, and felt sure he would meet her the next day. It was inevitable. As he went to bed he reminded himself that only a very short time ago she had been a schoolgirl, like his own daughter, learning her lessons, he remembered how much there was of shyness and constraint in her laughter, in her way of conversing with a stranger—it was probably the first time in her life that she found herself alone, and in a situation in which men could follow her and watch her, and speak to her, all the time with a secret aim she could not fail to divine. He recalled her slender, delicate neck, her fine gray eyes.

"And yet there's something pathetic about her," he thought to himself as he fell asleep.


II.

A week had passed since the beginning of their acquaintance. It was a holiday. Indoors it was stuffy, but the dust rose in clouds out of doors, and people's hats blew off. It was a parching day and Gurov kept going to the outdoor café for fruit drinks and ices to offer Anna Sergeyevna. The heat was overpowering.

In the evening, when the wind had dropped, they walked to the pier to see the steamer come in. There were a great many people strolling about the landing-place; some, bunches of flowers in their hands, were meeting friends. Two pecularities of the smart Yalta crowd stood out distinctly— the elderly ladies all tried to dress very youthfully, and there seemed to be an inordinate number of generals about.

Owing to the roughness of the sea the steamer arrived late, after the sun had gone down, and it had to maneuver for some time before it could get alongside the pier. Anna Sergeyevna scanned the steamer and passengers through her lorgnette, as if looking for someone she knew, and when she turned to Gurov her eyes were glistening. She talked a great deal, firing off abrupt questions and forgetting immediately what it was she had wanted to know. Then she lost her lorgnette in the crush.

The smart crowd began dispersing, features could no longer be made out, the wind had quite dropped, and Gurov and Anna Sergeyevna stood there as if waiting for someone else to come off the steamer. Anna Sergeyevna had fallen silent, every now and then smelling her flowers, but not looking at Gurov.

"It's turned out a fine evening," he said. "What shall we do? We might go for a drive."

She made no reply.

He looked steadily at her and suddenly took her in his arms and kissed her lips, and the fragrance and the dampness of the flowers closed round him, but the next moment he looked behind him in alarm—had anyone seen them?

"Let's go to your room," he murmured.

And they walked off together, very quickly.

Her room was stuffy and smelt of some scent she had bought in the Japanese shop. Gurov looked at her, thinking to himself: "How full of strange encounters life is!" He could remember carefree, good-natured women who were exhilarated by love-making and grateful to him for the happiness he gave them, however short-lived; and there had been others—his wife among them—whose caresses were insincere, affected, hysterical, mixed up with a great deal of quite unnecessary talk, and whose expression seemed to say that all this was just not lovemaking or passion, but something much more significant; then there had been two or three beautiful, cold women, over whose features flitted a predatory expression, betraying a determination to wring from life more than it could give, women no longer in their first youth, capricious, irrational, despotic, brainless, and when Gurov had cooled to these, their beauty aroused in him nothing but repulsion, and the lace trimming on their underclothes reminded him of fish-scales.

But here the timidity and awkwardness of youth and inexperience were still apparent; and there was a feeling of embarrassment in the atmosphere, as if someone had just knocked at the door. Anna Sergeyevna, "the lady with the dog," seemed to regard the affair as something very special, very serious, as if she had become a fallen woman, an attitude he found odd and disconcerting. Her features lengthened and drooped, and her long hair hung mournfully on either side of her face. She assumed a pose of dismal meditation, like a re-pentant sinner in some classical painting.

"It isn't right," she said. "You will never respect me anymore."

On the table was a watermelon. Gurov cut himself a slice from it and began slowly eating it. At least half an hour passed in silence.

Anna Sergeyevna was very touching, revealing the purity of a decent, naïve woman who had seen very little of life. The solitary candle burning on the table scarcely lit up her face, but it was obvious that her heart was heavy.

"Why should I stop respecting you?" asked Gurov. "You don't know what you're saying."

"May God forgive me!" she exclaimed, and her eyes filled with tears. "It's terrible."

"No need to seek to justify yourself."

"How can I justify myself? I'm a wicked, fallen woman, I despise myself and have not the least thought of self-justifi-cation. It isn't my husband I have deceived, it's myself. And not only now, I have been deceiving myself for ever so long. My husband is no doubt an honest, worthy man, but he's a flunky. I don't know what it is he does at his office, but I know he's a flunky. I was only twenty when I married him, and I was devoured by curiosity, I wanted something higher. I told myself that there must be a different kind of life I wanted to live, to live….I was burning with curiosity…you'll never understand that but I swear to God I could no longer control myself, nothing could hold me back, I told my husband I was ill, and I came here….And I started going about like one possessed, like a madwoman…and now I have become an ordinary, worthless woman, and everyone has the right to despise me."

Gurov listened to her, bored to death. The naïve accents, the remorse, all was so unexpected, so out of place. But for the tears in her eyes, she might have been jesting or play-acting.

"I don't understand," he said gently. "What is it you want?"

She hid her face against his breast and pressed closer to him.

"Do believe me, I implore you to believe me," she said. "I love all that is honest and pure in life, vice is revolting to me, I don't know what I'm doing. The common people say they are snared by the Devil. And now I can say I've been snared by the Devil, too."

"Come, come," he murmured.

He gazed into her fixed, terrified eyes, kissed her, and soothed her with gentle affectionate words, and gradually she calmed down and regained her cheerfulness. Soon they were laughing together again.

When, a little later, they went out, there was not a soul on the promenade, the town and its cypresses looked dead, but the sea was still roaring as it dashed against the beach.

A solitary fishing-boat tossed on the waves, its lamps blinking sleepily.

They found a carriage and drove to Oreanda.

"I discovered your name in the hall, just now," said Gurov, "written up on the board. Von Diederitz. Is your husband a German?"

"No. His grandfather was, I think, but he belongs to the Orthodox Church himself."

When they got out of the carriage at Oreanda they sat down on a bench not far from the church, and looked down at the sea, without talking. Yalta could be dimly discerned through the morning mist, and white clouds rested motionless on the summits of the mountains. Not a leaf stirred, the grasshoppers chirruped, and the monotonous hollow roar of the sea came up on them, speaking of peace, of the eternal sleep lying in wait for us all. The sea had roared like this long before there was any Yalta or Oreanda, it was roaring now, and it would go on roaring, just as indifferently and hollowly, when we had passed away. And it may be that in this continuity, this utter indifference to the life and death of each of us lies hidden the pledge of our eternal salvation, of the continuous movement of life on earth, of the continuous movement toward perfection.

Side by side with a young woman, who looked so exquisite in the early light, soothed and enchanted by the sight of all this magical beauty—sea, mountains, clouds and the vast expanse of the sky—Gurov told himself that, when you came to think of it, everything in the world is beautiful really, everything but our own thoughts and actions, when we lose sight of the higher aims of life, and of our dignity as human beings.

Someone approached them—a watchman, probably—looked at them and went away. And there was something mysterious and beautiful even in this. The steamer from Feodosia could be seen coming towards the pier, lit up by the dawn, its lamps out.

"There's dew on the grass," said Anna Sergeyevna, breaking the silence.

"Yes. Time to go home."

They went back to the town.

After this they met every day at noon on the promenade, lunching and dining together, going for walks, and admiring the sea. She complained of sleeplessness, of palpitations, asked the same questions over and over again, alternately surrendering to jealousy and the fear that he did not really respect her. And often, when there was nobody in sight in the square or the park, he would draw her to him and kiss her passionately. The utter idleness, these kisses in broad daylight, accompanied by furtive glances and the fear of discovery, the heat, the smell of the sea, and the idle, smart, well-fed people continually crossing their field of vision, seemed to have given him a new lease on life. He told Anna Sergeyevna she was beautiful and seductive, made love to her with impetuous passion, and never left her side, while she was always pensive, always trying to force from him the admission that he did not respect her, that he did not love her a bit, that he considered her just an ordinary woman. Almost every night they drove out of town, to Oreanda, the waterfall, or some other beauty-spot. And these excursions were invariably a success, each contributing fresh impressions of majestic beauty.

All this time they kept expecting her husband to arrive. But a letter came in which he told his wife that he was having trouble with his eyes, and implored her to come home as soon as possible. Anna Sergeyevna made hasty preparations for leaving.

"It's a good thing I'm going," she said to Gurov. "It's the intervention of fate."

She left Yalta in a carriage, and he went with her as far as the railway station. The drive took nearly a whole day. When she got into the express train, after the second bell had been rung, she said:

"Let me have one last look at you....One last look. That's right."

She did not weep, but was mournful, and seemed ill, the muscles of her cheeks twitching.

"I shall think of you...I shall think of you all the time," she said. "God bless you! Think kindly of me. We are parting forever, it must be so, because we ought never to have met. Good-bye—God bless you."

The train steamed rapidly out of the station, its lights soon disappearing, and a minute later even the sound it made was silenced, as if everything were conspiring to bring this sweet oblivion, this madness, to an end as quickly as possible. And Gurov, standing alone on the platform and gazing into the dark distance, listened to the shrilling of the grasshoppers and the humming of the telegraph wires, with a feeling that he had only just awakened. And he told himself that this had been just one more of the many adventures in his life, and that it, too, was over, leaving nothing but a memory....He was moved and sad, and felt a slight remorse. After all, this young woman whom he would never again see had not been really happy with him. He had been friendly and affectionate with her, but in his whole behaviour, in the tones of his voice, in his very caresses, there had been a shade of irony, the insulting indulgence of the fortunate male, who was, moreover, almost twice her age. She had insisted in calling him good, remarkable, high-minded. Evidently he had appeared to her different from his real self, in a word he had involuntarily deceived her....

There was an autumnal feeling in the air, and the evening was chilly.

"It's time for me to be going north, too," thought Gurov, as he walked away from the platform. "High time!"

III

When he got back to Moscow it was beginning to look like winter; the stoves were heated every day, and it was still dark when the children got up to go to school and drank their tea, so that the nurse had to light the lamp for a short time. Frost had set in. When the first snow falls, and one goes for one's first sleigh-ride, it is pleasant to see the white ground, the white roofs; one breathes freely and lightly, and remembers the days of one's youth. The ancient lime-trees and birches, white with hoarfrost, have a good-natured look, they are closer to the heart than cypresses and palms, and beneath their branches one is no longer haunted by the memory of mountains and the sea.

Gurov had always lived in Moscow, and he returned to Moscow on a fine frosty day, and when he put on his fur-lined overcoat and thick gloves, and sauntered down Petro-vka Street, and when, on Saturday evening, he heard the church bells ringing, his recent journey and the places he had visited lost their charm for him. He became gradually immersed in Moscow life, reading with avidity three newspapers a day, while declaring he never read Moscow newspapers on principle. Once more he was caught up in a whirl of restaurants, clubs, banquets, and celebrations, once more glowed with the flattering consciousness that well-known lawyers and actors came to his house, that he played cards in the Medical Club opposite a professor. He could once again eat a whole serving of Moscow Fish Stew served in a pan.

He had believed that in a month's time Anna Sergeyevna would be nothing but a vague memory, and that hereafter, with her wistful smile, she would only occasionally appear to him in dreams, like others before her. But the month was now well over and winter was in full swing, and all was as clear in his memory as if he had parted with Anna Sergeyevna only the day before. And his recollections grew ever more insistent. When the voices of his children at their lessons reached him in his study through the evening stillness, when he heard a song, or the sounds of a music-box in a restaurant, when the wind howled in the chimney, it all came back to him: early morning on the pier, the misty mountains, the steamer from Feodosia, the kisses. He would pace up and down his room for a long time, smiling at his memories, and then memory turned into dreaming, and what had happened mingled in his imagination with what was going to happen. Anna Sergeyevna did not come to him in his dreams, she accompanied him everywhere, like his shadow, following him everywhere he went. When he closed his eyes, she seemed to stand before him in the flesh, still lovelier, younger, tenderer than she had really been, and looking back, he saw himself, too, as better than he had been in Yalta. In the evenings she looked out at him from the bookshelves, the fireplace, the corner, he could hear her breathing, the sweet rustle of her skirts. In the streets he followed women with his eyes, to see if there were any like her....

He began to feel an overwhelming desire to share his memories with someone. But he could not speak of his love at home, and outside his home who was there for him to confide in? Not the tenants living in his house, and certainly not his colleagues at the bank. And what was there to tell? Was it love that he had felt? Had there been anything exquisite, poetic, anything instructive or even amusing about his relations with Anna Sergeyevna? He had to content himself with uttering vague generalizations about love and women, and nobody guessed what he meant, though his wife's dark eyebrows twitched as she said:

"The role of a coxcomb doesn't suit you a bit, Dimitry."

One evening, leaving the Medical Club with one of his card-partners, a government official, he could not refrain from remarking:

"If you only knew what a charming woman I met in Yalta!"

The official got into his sleigh, and just before driving off, turned and called out:

"Dmitry Dmitrich!"

"Yes?"

"You were quite right, you know—the sturgeon was just a *leetle* off."

These words, in themselves so commonplace, for some reason infuriated Gurov, seemed to him humiliating, gross. What savage manners, what people! What wasted evenings, what tedious, empty days! Frantic card-playing, gluttony, drunkenness, perpetual talk always about the same thing. The greater part of one's time and energy went on business that was no use to anyone, and on discussing the same thing over and over again, and there was nothing to show for it all but a stunted wingless existence and a round of trivialities, and there was nowhere to escape to, you might as well be in a madhouse or a convict settlement.

Gurov lay awake all night, raging, and went about the whole of the next day with a headache. He slept badly on the succeeding nights, too, sitting up in bed, thinking, or pacing the floor of his room. He was sick of his children, sick of the bank, felt not the slightest desire to go anywhere or talk about anything.

When the Christmas holidays came, he packed his things, telling his wife he had to go to Petersburg in the interests of a certain young man, and set off for the town of S. To what end? He hardly knew himself. He only knew that he must see Anna Sergeyevna, must speak to her, arrange a meeting, if possible.

He arrived at S. in the morning and engaged the best suite in the hotel, which had a carpet of gray military frieze, and a dusty inkpot on the table, surmounted by a headless rider, holding his hat in his raised hand. The hall porter told him what he wanted to know: Von Diederitz had a house of his own in Staro-Goncharnaya Street. It wasn't far from the hotel, he lived on a grand scale, luxuriously, kept carriage-horses, the whole town knew him. The hall porter pronounced the name "Drideritz."

Gurov strolled over to Staro-Goncharnaya Street and discovered the house. In front of it was a long gray fence with inverted nails hammered into the tops of the palings.

"A fence like that is enough to make anyone want to run away," thought Gurov, looking at the windows of the house and the fence. He reasoned that since it was a holiday, Anna's husband would probably be at home. In any case it would be tactless to embarrass her by calling at the house. And a note might fall into the hands of the husband, and bring about catastrophe. The best thing would be to wait about on the chance of seeing her. And he walked up and down the street, hovering in the vicinity of the fence, watching for his chance. A beggar entered the gate, only to be attacked by dogs, then, an hour later, the faint, vague sounds of a piano reached his ears. That would be Anna Sergeyevna playing. Suddenly the front door opened and an old woman came out, followed by a familiar white Pomeranian. Gurov tried to call to it, but his heart beat violently, and in his agitation he could not remember its name.

He walked on, hating the gray fence more and more, and now ready to tell himself irately that Anna Sergeyevna had forgotten him, had already, perhaps, found distraction in another—what could be more natural in a young woman who had to look at this accursed fence from morning to night? He went back to his hotel and sat on the sofa in his suite for some time, not knowing what to do, then he ordered dinner, and after dinner, had a long sleep.

"What a foolish, restless business," he thought, waking up and looking towards the dark windowpanes. It was evening by now. "Well, I've had my sleep out. And what am I to do in the night?"

He sat up in bed, covered by the cheap gray quilt, which reminded him of a hospital blanket, and in his vexation he fell to taunting himself.

"You and your lady with a dog … there's adventure for you! See what you get for your pains."

On his arrival at the station that morning he had noticed a poster announcing in enormous letters the first performance at the local theatre of *The Geisha*.[4] Remembering this; he got up and made for the theatre.

"It's highly probable that she goes to first nights," he told himself. The theatre was full. It was a typical provincial theatre, with a mist collecting over the chandeliers, and the crowd in the gallery fidgeting noisily. In the first row of the stalls the local dandies stood waiting for the curtain to go up, their hands clasped behind them. There, in the front seat of the governor's box, sat the governor's daughter, wearing a boa, the governor himself hiding modestly behind the drapes, so that only his hands were visible. The curtain stirred, the orchestra took a long time tuning up their instruments. Gurov's eyes roamed eagerly over the audience as they filed in and occupied their seats.

Anna Sergeyevna came in, too. She seated herself in the third row of the stalls, and when Gurov's glance fell on her, his heart seemed to stop, and he knew in a flash that the whole world contained no one nearer or dearer to him, no one more important to his happiness. This little woman, lost in the provincial crowd, in no way remarkable, holding a silly lorgnette in her hand, now filled his whole life, was his grief, his joy, all that he desired. Lulled by the sounds coming from the wretched orchestra, with its feeble, amateurish violinists, he thought how beautiful she was ... thought and dreamed....

Anna Sergeyevna was accompanied by a tall, round-shouldered young man with small whiskers, who nodded at every step before taking the seat beside her and seemed to be continually bowing to someone. This must be her husband, whom, in a fit of bitterness, at Yalta, she had called a "flunky." And there really was something of a lackey's servility in his lanky figure, his side-whiskers, and the little bald spot on the top of his head. And he smiled sweetly, and the badge of some scientific society gleaming in his buttonhole was like the number on a footman's livery.

The husband went out to smoke in the first interval, and she was left alone in her seat. Gurov, who had taken a seat in the stalls, went up to her and said in a trembling voice, with a forced smile: "How d'you do?"

She glanced up at him and turned pale, then looked at him again in alarm, unable to believe her eyes, squeezing her fan and lorgnette in one hand, evidently struggling to overcome a feeling of faintness. Neither of them said a word. She sat there, and he stood beside her, disconcerted by her embarrassment, and not daring to sit down. The violins and flutes sang out as they were tuned, and there was a tense sensation in the atmosphere, as if they were being watched from all the boxes. At last she got up and moved rapidly towards one of the exits. He followed her and they wandered aimlessly along corridors, up and down stairs; figures flashed by in the uniforms of legal officials, high-school teachers and civil servants, all wearing badges; ladies, coats hanging from pegs flashed by; there was a sharp draft, bringing with it an odor of cigarette butts. And Gurov, whose heart was beating violently, thought:

"What on earth are all these people, this orchestra for? . . ."

The next minute he suddenly remembered how, after seeing Anna Sergeyevna off that evening at the station, he had told himself that all was over, and they would never meet again. And how far away the end seemed to be now!

She stopped on a dark narrow staircase over which was a notice bearing the inscription "To the upper circle."

"How you frightened me!" she said, breathing heavily, still pale and half-stunned. "Oh, how you frightened me! I'm almost dead! Why did you come? Oh, why?"

"But, Anna," he said, in low, hasty tones. "But, Anna. . . . Try to understand . . . do try. . . ."

She cast him a glance of fear, entreaty, love, and then gazed at him steadily, as if to fix his features firmly in her memory.

"I've been so unhappy," she continued, taking no notice of his words. "I could think of nothing but you the whole time, I lived on the thoughts of you. I tried to forget—why, oh, why did you come?"

On the landing above them were two schoolboys, smoking and looking down, but Gurov did not care, and, drawing Anna Sergeyevna towards him, began kissing her face, her lips, her hands.

"What are you doing, oh, what are you doing?" she said in horror, drawing back. "We have both gone mad. Go away this very night, this moment. . . . By all that is sacred, I implore you. . . . Somebody is coming."

Someone was ascending the stairs.

"You must go away," went on Anna Sergeyevna in a whisper. "D'you hear me, Dmitry Dmitrich? I'll come to you in Moscow. I have never been happy, I am unhappy now, and I shall never be happy—never! Do not make me suffer still more! I will come to you in Moscow, I swear it! And now we must part! My dear one, my kind one, my darling, we must part."

She pressed his hand and hurried down the stairs, looking back at him continually, and her eyes showed that she was in truth unhappy. Gurov stood where he was for a short time, listening, and when all was quiet, went to look for his coat, and left the theatre.

IV

And Anna Sergeyevna began going to Moscow to see him. Every two or three months she left the town of S., telling her husband that she was going to consult a specialist on female diseases, and her husband believed her and did not believe her. In Moscow she always stayed at the Slavyanski Bazaar, sending a man in a red cap to Gurov the moment she arrived. Gurov went to her, and no one in Moscow knew anything about it.

One winter morning he went to see her as usual (the messenger had been to him the evening before, but had not found him at home). His daughter was with him, for her school was on the way and he thought he might as well see her to it.

"It is forty degrees," said Gurov to his daughter, "and yet it is snowing. You see it is only above freezing close to the ground, the temperature in the upper layers of the atmosphere is quite different."

"Why doesn't it ever thunder in winter, Papa?"

He explained this, too. As he was speaking, he kept reminding himself that he was going to a rendezvous and that not a living soul knew about it, or, probably, ever would. He led a double life—one in public, in the sight of all whom it concerned, full of conventional truth and conventional deception, exactly like the lives of his friends and acquaintances, and another which flowed in secret. And, owing to some strange, possibly quite accidental chain of circumstances, everything that was important, interesting, essential, everything about which he was sincere and never deceived himself, everything that composed the kernel of his life, went on in secret, while everything that was false in him, everything that composed the husk in which he hid himself and the truth which was in him—his work at the bank, discussions at the club, his "lower race," his attendance at anniversary celebrations with his wife—was on the surface. He began to judge others by himself, no longer believing what he saw, and always assuming that the real, the only interesting life of every individual goes on as under cover of night, secretly. Every individual existence revolves around mystery, and perhaps that is the chief reason that all cultivated individuals insisted so strongly on the respect due to personal secrets.

After leaving his daughter at the door of her school Gurov set off for the Slavyanski-Bazaar. Taking off his overcoat in the lobby, he went upstairs and knocked softly on the door. Anna Sergeyevna, wearing the gray dress he liked most, exhausted by her journey and by suspense, had been expecting him since the evening before. She was pale and looked at him without smiling, but was in his arms almost before he was fairly in the room. Their kiss was lingering, prolonged, as if they had not met for years.

"Well, how are you?" he asked. "Anything new?"

"Wait, I'll tell you in a minute....I can't. . . ."

She could not speak, because she was crying. Turning away, she held her handkerchief to her eyes.

"I'll wait till she's had her cry out," he thought, and sank into a chair.

He rang for tea, and a little later, while he was drinking it, she was still standing there, her face to the window. She wept from emotion, from her bitter consciousness of the sadness of their life; they could only see one another in secret, hiding from people, as if they were thieves. Was not their life a broken one?

"Don't cry," he said.

It was quite obvious to him that this love of theirs would not soon come to an end, and that no one could say when this end would be. Anna Sergeyevna loved him ever more fondly, worshipped him, and there would have been no point in telling her that one day it must end. Indeed, she would not have believed him.

He moved over and took her by the shoulders, intending to caress her, to make a joke, but suddenly he caught sight of himself in the looking-glass.

His hair was already beginning to turn gray. It struck him as strange that he should have aged so much in the last few years, have lost so much of his looks. The shoulders on which his hands lay were warm and quivering. He felt a pity for this life, still so warm and exquisite, but probably soon to fade and droop like his own. Why did she love him so? Women had always believed him different from what he really was, had loved in him not himself but the man their imagination pictured him, a man they had sought for eagerly all their lives. And afterwards when they discovered their mistake, they went on loving him just the same. And not one of them had ever been happy with him. Time had passed, he had met one woman after another, become intimate with each, parted with each, but had never loved. There had been all sorts of things between them, but never love.

And only now, when he was gray-haired, had he fallen in love properly, thoroughly, for the first time in his life.

He and Anna Sergeyevna loved one another as people who are very close and intimate, as husband and wife, as dear friends love one another. It seemed to them that fate had intended them for one another, and they could not understand why she should have a husband, and he a wife. They were like two migrating birds, the male and the female, who had been caught and put into separate cages. They forgave one another all that they were ashamed of in the past and in the present, and felt that this love of theirs had changed them both.

Formerly, in moments of melancholy, he had consoled himself by the first argument that came into his head, but now arguments were nothing to him, he felt profound pity, desired to be sincere, tender.

"Stop crying, my dearest," he said. "You've had your cry, now stop....Now let us have a talk, let us try and think what we are to do."

Then they discussed their situation for a long time, trying to think how they could get rid of the necessity for hiding, deception, living in different towns, being so long without meeting. How were they to shake off these intolerable fetters?

"How? How?" he repeated, clutching his head. "How?"

And it seemed to them that they were within an inch of arriving at a decision, and that then a new, beautiful life would begin. And they both realized that the end was still far, far away, and that the hardest, the most complicated part was only just beginning.

1   A fashionable seaside resort in the Crimea.
2   Certain progressive intellectuals omitted the hard sign after consonants in writing. They anticipated the reform in the Russian alphabet introduced later. Here used rather as emancipated affectation.
3   District administration.
4   An operetta by the English composer Sidney Jones (1897).

# Of Mystery
# There Is No End

## Leonard Michaels

Traffic might move at any moment. He might still get to the dentist on time, but Nachman was pessimistic and he assumed that he would miss his appointment. He pictured himself apologizing to Gudrun, the dentist's assistant, a pale Norwegian woman in her forties with white-blond hair. Nachman could almost hear his ingratiating tone. He was begging Gudrun to forgive him, swearing that it would never happen again, when he felt himself being watched. He looked to his left. In the car next to his, a young woman was staring at him. She looked away immediately and pretended to chat on a cell phone, as though indifferent to Nachman, who now stared at her. He saw heavy makeup and chemical red hair. She was smoking a cigarette and tapping the steering wheel with her thumb, keeping time to music on her car radio. Nachman imagined reaching into her car, snatching away her cell phone and cigarette, turning off her radio, and ordering her to sit still. She would soon be reduced to quivering lunacy. Drivers in Los Angeles shoot one another for no reason, let alone for rude staring.

Of course, Nachman would never have shot anybody. He pitied the woman who encumbered her head with cell phones, cigarettes, popular music, and unnatural colors. Compared to her, Nachman was a sublime being. He could sit alone for hours in his office with only a pencil and a notebook. Thinking. In fact, there was a pencil and a notebook in the glove compartment. Nachman's car could be his office. He would do math problems. Millions were stalled and rotting in their cars in Los Angeles, but Nachman had internal resources.

He leaned toward the glove compartment and, just as he touched the release button, his eye was drawn by a flash of black hair. He looked. Adele Novgorad, the wife of Nachman's best and oldest friend, Norbert Novgorad, was standing on the sidewalk. Nachman wanted to call out her name, but hesitated. He was sure it was Adele, though she was turned away from him. Few people in Los Angeles had such wonderfully black hair and skin so white. But she was talking to a man who had an unusually large and intimidating mustache, and they stood close together—too close facing each other in front of a motel, about ten yards a from Nachman's car. Horns blared behind Nachman. He heard the horns, but they meant nothing. Adele and the man had begun kissing.

The horns blared again and again and at last they pierced Nachman's trance. He looked away from Adele to the road, but for Nachman, still shocked by what he had seen, the avenue, the traffic, the buildings were all meaningless. He grasped the steering wheel. Fairfax Avenue was clear for a thousand yards straight ahead, but he didn't step on the gas pedal. He looked back at Adele. She had stopped kissing the man, though she still clung to him; the man had now heard the horns and was looking over her shoulder at Nachman's car. When their eyes met, Nachman stepped on the gas and released the clutch. In the rearview mirror, he saw Adele separate from the man. He was pointing at Nachman's car. Adele looked. Having seen too much, Nachman had been seen.

Driving south down Fairfax, Nachman felt something like a thrill of departure, as when a boat leaves the shore, but the thrill was unpleasant. He seemed to be departing from himself, or from everything familiar to himself. Through the blur of feeling, a voice spoke to him: "You must tell Norbert what you saw on Fairfax Avenue." It was Nachman's own voice, commanding and severe.

He could drive to the community college where Norbert was a professor. And then what? Interrupt a lecture or a department meeting to tell him that he had seen Adele kissing somebody? How ridiculous. Besides, if he told Norbert, Adele would hate him. She, too, was his friend. She had invited Nachman to dinner many times, and she always gave him a tight hug and a kiss when he arrived and again when he left, pressing her warm lips against his cheek. She cooked special dishes for Nachman. To please her, he cried out with pleasure at the first bite, and when she looked gratified he took more delight in her expression than he did in the food. With her cooking and hugs and kisses, Adele made Nachman feel that he was very important to her. He liked her enormously. He also got a kick out of her smile, which was usually accompanied by a frown, as if happiness were a pleasant form of melancholy. Nachman sometimes wanted to lean across the dinner table and kiss the lines in her brow. He suddenly heard himself speak again, in a cruel voice, as if he were a stranger to himself and had no regard for his own feelings about Adele: "You must tell Norbert what you saw on Fairfax Avenue."

Nachman hammered the dashboard with his fist and shouted an obscenity. In the twenty-first century, in Los Angeles, a great city of cars where no conceivable depravity wasn't already boring to highschool kids, Nachman, a grown man, found himself agonized by an ancient moral dilemma.

Was it his duty to tell Norbert or to protect Adele? Would it make any difference if he told Norbert? Yes, it would make a difference. The friendship would be ruined. Nachman forced himself to ask: Did he want to hurt his friend Norbert? There was no reason to tell him, unless he wanted to hurt him. People who told unbearable news to friends, as if it were their duty, and then felt very good about themselves while their friends felt miserable—Nachman was not like those people.

Besides, to feel good about oneself was important only to narcissists, not to Nachman. Nachman loved his friend Norbert and would sooner cut off his own arm than hurt him just to feel good about himself. In the righteous fervor of his thinking, Nachman forgot about his dental appointment.

He drove to the ocean and turned toward Malibu. He barely noticed that he had passed his house. After a while, he saw a place to stop. He parked close to the beach and left his car. He trudged along the sand without taking off his shoes. The ocean was a sheet of glinting metallic brilliance. Gulls were dark blades soaring in the white glare of the afternoon sun. For the gulls, light was no different from air. For Nachman, the difference between one thing and another was the most serious consideration in life. The gulls brought this home to him with terrible poignancy. He remembered his first lesson in mathematics, when he had learned about differences.

After his parents had divorced, when Nachman was five, and his father had moved out, Nachman's mother's aunt, Natasha Lurie, had come to stay. She was a small elderly woman from St. Petersburg, Russia, and had been a well-known mathematician in her youth. She decided to teach Nachman mathematics, and began the lesson by asking him, in a soft tired voice, to write the word "mathematics." Nachman wrote it phonetically, with an "a" in the middle. Natasha, who reminded him of clothes hanging on a line, susceptible to the least touch of the wind, took Nachman's pencil out of his hand. Pinching the pencil between her own skinny white fingers, she dragged the eraser back and forth on the paper, back and forth until the "a" was obliterated. Then she drew a round and perfect "e," pushing the pencil point into the fibre of the paper and pulling the shape of the letter, like a small worm, slowly into view. More than four decades later, trudging on the beach in Malibu, Nachman saw again the red rims of Aunt Natasha's ancient eyes. She looked at Nachman to see if he understood. The lesson had had little to do with spelling or with mathematics. She had taught him that there was a right way. It applied to everything.

He thought of Adele smooching on Fairfax Avenue as he trudged back to his car and drove to Santa Monica and then to his house. When he opened the door, Nachman heard the phone ringing. It continued to ring while he looked through the mail he had collected from the box attached to the front of his house. He entered his study and sat down at his rolltop desk. The phone continued ringing.

Nachman put the bills in one pile and dropped junk mail, unopened, into a wastebasket. Then he opened his personal mail. He found a request: Would Professor Nachman read the manuscript of a proposed mathematics textbook? It was being considered for publication by a major East Coast firm. The job would take many hours. Nachman would be paid five hundred dollars for his opinion and suggestions. It wasn't much money, but he supposed he was expected to feel honored by the request. He then found two invitations. One was to a conference on mathematical physics, in Indiana. Why had they invited

Nachman? It wasn't his specialty. The appropriate mathematicians had probably turned them down. The second invitation was for a defense job. It had to do with antiballistic-missile systems and would pay ten times what Nachman was making at the Institute of Mathematics. It was a job, Nachman guessed, that was held only by third-rate mathematicians and by spies. Anti-ballistic missiles, indeed. Nachman felt insulted. What a terrible day. The phone was ringing. Nachman went to the bathroom and swallowed an aspirin. He then went to the bedroom and sat on the edge of his bed and took off his shoes and socks. The phone on his night table was ringing.

Late afternoon light, filtered by the leaves of an avocado tree outside his bedroom window, glowed on the pine floor and trembled like the surface of a pond. It was a beautiful and deeply pleasing light, but the roots of the magnificent avocado tree had been undermining the concrete foundation of Nachman's house for years. He thought about that almost every day. Sooner or later, he would have to choose between the tree and the resale value of the house.

There was sand in his shoes and socks, and sand between his toes. On the night table beside the bed, the phone was ringing. Nachman lay down on his back and placed his right forearm across his eyes. Let the foundation be torn apart. Let the house fall down. Let the phone ring. Nachman would sleep. Let the phone ring....It was impossible to sleep. Nachman sat up on the edge of his bed and lifted the receiver. He didn't say hello.

"It's me," she said.

"Goodbye," Nachman said.

"Don't you dare hang up. You knew it was me. You could hear the ringing. You're the only person in California who doesn't have an answering machine. You heard the phone. Why didn't you pick it up?"

"Between you and me, Adele, a certain subject does not exist."

"If any subject doesn't exist, no subject exists."

"So we have no subjects."

"I caused you pain. Is that it?"

"I live a simple life. Like a peasant. I go to work. After dinner I go to sleep. I have no interest in adventures."

"We have different needs. I'm not you, Nachman. And you are not me. I couldn't live without an answering machine or a television set."

"O.K., let's leave it at that. I have a headache."

"I don't want to leave it at that. I want to understand. I have great respect for your opinions."

"Adele, I am not in the mood for a confessional orgy. I will say only this—I don't believe that experience, for its own sake, is the highest value. Kissing in the street, in the middle of Los Angeles ... For God's sake. How could you?"

"You saw me kissing a guy. Was it a threat to your peasant simplicity?"

"In the middle of the afternoon, on Fairfax Avenue, with the *bubees* and *zeydes* walking home with grocery bags. There are limits."

"I think you mean morals."

"O.K., morals. Yes, morals. You have something against morals?" Nachman heard himself shouting and felt his breath coming faster.

"Morals-schmorals. It sounds to me like you think I did something to you personally."

"I saw you kissing some guy who isn't Norbert, my best friend, who happens to be your husband. It was a spectacle of irresponsible lust performed in public, in my face—Norbert's best friend."

"Nachman, get ahold of yourself! How the fuck would I know that Norbert's best friend was stopped in traffic, twenty feet away?"

"You trivialize my feelings."

"What is it that you feel? Tell me exactly."

"This minute, talking to you, I feel exactly as if I were betraying Norbert."

"Oh, please. Every time you look at me, you betray Norbert. When I stroll down Wilshire Boulevard, Norbert is betrayed sixty times a minute. I answer the door to the postman, Norbert has horns. This is California, not Saudi Arabia. I'm a woman on display, front and back. Do you know it's been said that a modern woman can neither dress nor undress."

"Who said it?"

"I don't know, but it's true. Look, all that matters is you and me, Nachman—we're friends. Our conversation is not a betrayal of anybody. Aren't we friends? I thought we were friends."

Adele was crying.

"Of course," Nachman said, his voice hoarse, on the verge of failure. "Nachman, are you in love with me?" Adele said. "Is that the real problem here?"

"I love many people."

"Liar. You love your mother in San Diego, and you never talk about your father or your colleagues or the women you date. Anyhow, I said 'in love with me.'"

"What does that have to do with anything?"

"It has to do with everything. Norbert is the injured party, not you. Don't you hear yourself?"

"What should I hear?"

"Don't be a mystery to yourself, Nachman. Maybe we all walk in darkness, shadows, mystery—I wouldn't deny it—but you must try to understand. Of mystery there is no end. Of clarity there is precious little."

"Adele, you're raving. Stop it."

She spoke in a rush, sniffling and sobbing, "O.K., I'll stop, but I want to make things clear to you. The telephone is no damn good. Let's meet at Calendar's, near the La Brea Tar Pits. It's a few blocks from my office. I go there for lunch. One o'clock tomorrow. If you don't show up, Nachman, I'll understand that you didn't want to betray Norbert. But please do show up."

After the phone call, Nachman felt better. Nothing had actually changed, and yet he could think more liberally about what hadn't changed.

He continued to sit on the edge of his bed. He didn't want to move. It seemed he could still hear Adele's unmelodious voice, which had been made ragged by cigarettes. Adele had urged him to examine his feelings, but he didn't care to know too much about what he felt. After all, as soon as you know what you feel, you feel something else. No. There would be no such examination. It was enough that he felt cheered by Adele's phone call. He admired her daring. He was reminded of how he liked her sluggish, heavy carriage. She walked as if she had large breasts, though they were average, proportionate to her height, which was about five feet five inches. Her hips seemed to lock slowly, and then reluctantly to unlock as she walked, toes pointed outward. Nachman wanted, mindlessly, to hug her.

O.K., he thought, energized, returning to himself, the moral being. Look at the issue analytically, from Adele's point of view. As Adele had said, people have different needs. So let's be fair to Adele, a green-eyed Hungarian woman with considerable intelligence and nice hips. It was obvious, Nachman suddenly realized, that the unrelenting repetitiousness of domestic life was destroying Adele. So the poor woman had been unfaithful. What was infidelity, anyhow? What was it precisely that Adele might have done? Let's get that straight. She kissed a man? Big deal. Perhaps she had sexual intercourse? Oh, who cares? It was an imaginative experience, a mental tonic, like a trip to Paris, except of course you don't bring back photographs of yourself in a motel room performing fellatio to show your friends. But who cares? With stunning visionary force, a picture burst into Nachman's mind. Adele was naked, lying on her back with her wrists tied to bedposts. She smiled with vague, soporific satisfaction at Nachman, her green eyes glazed by a delirium of pleasure as she said, in her cigarette voice, "Morals-schmorals."

The picture vanished. Nachman looked down at his shoes, which he had dropped beside the bed. He felt an extraordinary need for ordinariness. His shoes were British. Hand-sewn, soft, reddish-brown leather. He'd worn them for years and he'd had them resoled and re-heeled at least three times. He kept them oiled. They were molded perfectly to the shape of his feet and so pliant they felt buttery. It occurred to Nachman, though he hadn't been thinking about it, that maybe Norbert already knew about Adele's lover.

If Norbert knew, and if Nachman told Norbert what he had seen, it might be grotesquely embarrassing. Boundaries are crucial to the integrity of relationships.

That settled it. He wouldn't tell Norbert and he wouldn't meet Adele for lunch. It was an enormous relief to have arrived at this understanding of his situation.

Traffic moved normally the next afternoon, so Nachman was on time when he parked his car in the lot near the La Brea Tar Pits. Calendar's was crowded. Waiters rushed down the aisles, with expressions of intense concentration, as if solving puzzles. There was ubiquitous chatter and laughter. Nachman looked around for Adele. When he saw her, he took a breath and started toward her table. She was wearing sandals, jeans, a celadon-green tank top, and a thin beaded necklace of primary colors. Beside her wine glass was a newspaper, which she pressed down with her hand as she read it. She glanced up as Nachman approached. She smiled, folded the newspaper, and dropped it beneath her chair. She continued smiling as Nachman sat down. He looked at her tank top and her necklace. He looked at her wedding ring, a barrel of dull yellow, and then at her watch. It had a large face, etched with black numerals, and a clear plastic band. Adele continued smiling. Nachman shook his head ruefully as he finally looked directly at her face.

Her black shining hair was pulled back severely, and tied with a red ribbon. She wore assertive poppy-red lipstick. In gold-framed glasses, her eyes, related to the color of her tank top though much brighter, accepted Nachman's attention, but he could see their uncertainty. Her smile became tentative. Quizzical.

"Order something," she said, unable to bear Nachman's silence.

"I don't want anything."

"Won't you have a glass of wine?" she implored, as if it would do her good if Nachman had a glass of wine. Her smile was weak.

"All right."

Adele raised her hand. A passing waiter stopped. Adele said, "Two more," pointing to her wine glass. The waiter nodded.

"I shouldn't have another," Adele said. "I have to work on a difficult case this afternoon. I hired a new assistant. A gay kid named Geoffrey Horley Harms. He has two degrees. Three names and two doctorates, can you believe it?" She paused, then said, "What are you thinking?"

"I wasn't thinking."

"You've never been married. You don't know what it's like."

Nachman looked around at the action in the restaurant and sighed.

Adele said, "This is going nowhere. Look at me, please. I want to talk to you. I wasn't raised by Protestants. I'm not a nice person. Do you follow me? I'm a very direct person."

"What are you talking about?"

"I want your full attention."

"O.K."

"I'm glad you saw me outside the motel."

"I was stuck in traffic. I'm sorry."

"Don't be sorry. I'm grateful. What you saw has been going on for a long time, but I could never tell anybody. If I told my girlfriends it would be unfair to Norbert. I'm bad, but I'm not evil. The guy you saw me with—Ivan—is from another life. I was in high school when we met. I was a kid. Ivan was already out of college, working. His mustache got to me. I don't know why. It made his face so fierce. But Ivan is very kind. He is in the insurance business, a claims adjuster. He doesn't live in Los Angeles. Sometimes he disappears for two or three years, then he phones me as if we were still together. As if I had never married. People stare at him because of his mustache. When he wears dark glasses he has no face, just a nose."

"Adele, what did you want to talk about?"

"I'm talking about it."

Nachman shut his eyes for a second, as if things would be different when he opened them. Nothing was different.

"Ivan phoned again a few days ago. Believe me, I was very clear and firm. I said I wouldn't meet him. I said that I felt bad about having done so in the past. I told him exactly how I felt. He started begging. I said no, no, no. The next day, he walked into my office. I almost fainted. He looked worse than shit. But the mustache was there, and old feelings were stirred. I was transported. What could I do? Even if I were a happily married woman, the old feelings would be there. I was helpless."

"Helpless? You?"

"Give me a break, Nachman."

"All right, you were helpless."

"So we went to a motel. Try to understand, Nachman. It's been going on for years, and I never told anyone. Motels. You wouldn't believe how many motels I've been in. Did you know that a lot of Indians are in the motel business?"

"I can't begin to tell you how interesting that is to me. Hindus or Muslims?"

"That's enough. I don't like being teased. So we went to the motel, a squalid dump at the edge of a trailer park."

A picture came. A motel room. The walls were water-stained and the paint was peeling away. Adele was standing beside a bed where a man lay. His eyes peered over a huge mustache, gazing at Adele as she stepped into her panties. She pulled them up, then plucked the material free of the crease in her behind. At that instant Nachman's wine glass was set before him. He reached too quickly and knocked the glass over. Wine splattered Adele.

Nachman said, "I'm sorry. I'm sorry."

Adele's tank top bore dark splotches like the shadows of maple leaves.

"They once threw stones," Adele said. "I'm getting off easy."

"What can I say?"

"I wanted you to listen. You don't have to say anything."

Adele swept her tongue across her teeth. A tiny dark-green shape, perhaps a piece of arugula, was plastered against her front tooth. Nachman ordered another glass of wine.

"If I hadn't seen you yesterday," he said, "nobody would ever have known.

"These things come out. I told Ivan it was over. I think he heard me this time. Why don't you order a sandwich or something? I already had a salad."

Nachman didn't want anything. Outside the restaurant, they stopped for a moment in the sunlight and looked up the avenue toward the County Museum.

"We should go there someday," Nachman said. "See the show and then go somewhere and have lunch."

"I'd like that."

Nachman kissed Adele on the cheek. She said, "Do you think I should ... now that I've told you?"

"Yes. Tell Norbert."

Nachman sounded principled, but he was already worried about whether Adele would ever invite him to dinner again. It would be a great loss if she decided that she had said too much and would prefer not to have Nachman around at the same time as her husband.

She had said that she was bad but not evil. Nachman wasn't sure what she'd meant. He supposed it had to do with Norbert's integrity. How he lived, consciously or not, in the eyes of other people. That was important to Adele. She wanted to protect Norbert. It was an aesthetic as well as a moral consideration. She'd had a long affair with Ivan, the mustache, but everything had ended in the motel. Nachman decided that, even bad, Adele remained lovable.

A week later, Norbert phoned. It was late evening. Nachman heard fatigue and displeasure in Norbert's voice. It sounded like anger or controlled pain. All that had troubled Nachman the week before rushed into his mind. He felt regret and shame. He braced internally, expecting to hear Norbert say, "You're a rat, Nachman. I'm furious with you."

Nachman hadn't told Norbert what he'd seen on Fairfax

Avenue, and he'd met Adele for lunch, thereby making himself complicitous. Nachman had agonized over those things, but to know what you're doing is not the same as fully appreciating the terribleness of it. Nachman pressed the receiver hard against his ear. He'd never felt worse. If punishment were available to people the moment they deserved it, Nachman would have been punished days before. He would then have been able to show Norbert the receipt. Nachman suddenly realized that every move a person made was to one degree or another criminal, and that there was a great shortage of punishment. These thoughts occurred in the instant before Norbert said, "Would you like to go for a drive? I bought a new car."

Norbert hadn't denounced him, thank God, but Nachman didn't look forward to the drive. Who knows what might be said? Who knows what lies Nachman might be obliged to tell? Nachman put down the receiver. His heart was beating quickly and heavily.

Fifteen minutes later, Norbert came by in his new car. It had a big engine and a dashboard like the flight panel of an airliner. Nachman had no idea what company made the car, and he wasn't curious. If the car nourished Norbert's spirit with fantasies of power, that was good.

"I like your new car," Nachman said. "Really great. Beautiful."

"Umm," Norbert said, as if distracted. Norbert drove out of the city along the San Diego Freeway. When a stretch of open road appeared, he stepped hard on the gas pedal. Nachman's spine pressed against the seat.

"Too fast, don't you think?" Nachman said.

"Are you serious?" There was contempt in Norbert's question. He continued. "I do a hundred and fifty in the desert."

Nachman glanced at the speedometer, saw that it read ninety-five, and then glanced at Norbert. What was he thinking? Norbert sat rigidly, staring down the road as if hypnotized by a point far off in the darkness. He was driving toward that point at a greater and greater speed. But he was getting no closer, because the point existed only within Norbert, and they would probably be dead before he reached it. Minutes passed with only the drone of the big engine. The road rushed toward them and was swept under the devouring hood. Nachman watched cars and trucks far ahead loom suddenly and vanish in a blur and whoosh. Norbert was driving well over a hundred miles per hour, speeding deeper into the night. Nachman was terrified but, trying to be a good friend, he said nothing to ruin Norbert's mood. Norbert needed to be in charge, needed to terrify Nachman. If Nachman demanded to be let out, Norbert would doubtless slow down and apologize. Maybe he was waiting for Nachman to lose his composure. Nachman forced himself to abide silently in terror. He deserved it; he accepted it. Part of him imagined that he wanted it.

Norbert seemed abruptly to soften, to relent. He continued to stare straight ahead and was no less self-absorbed, but he slowed the car, then made a careful turn and drove back toward Santa Monica.

"Let's have a drink," he said.

With no enthusiasm, Nachman said, "Do you know a place?"

"I know a place."

Norbert drove into Venice, and then to a bar in the middle of a long, poorly lit street. It was a dark room with low ceilings and sawdust on the floor. Surfer types were shooting pool in the rear. Their girlfriends, scrawny blond kids who looked much alike, sat on a bench against a wall and smoked. Men in motorcycle leathers were drinking beer at one end of the bar. Nachman would never have come to this place alone. But Norbert had a thick neck and broad shoulders. He was also fearless. He was descended from Russian peasants. Shrewd, strong, dark, stocky, he had never once been sick or had a toothache. He'd played rugby in college, a game where men hurtle against one another, as in American football, but with no girlish helmets or shoulder pads. The atmosphere of the bar, like driving fast at night, seemed to suit Norbert's mood. Nachman didn't want to stay, but he felt he owed his friend company the way convicts owe a debt to society. Norbert said, "I want a vodka Martini. You, too?"

Nachman nodded yes, though he would have preferred a Coke. The bartender sneered, saying "Vodka Martini?" as if Norbert had asked him to dance naked on a table. Norbert stared with no expression and said nothing, waiting for the bartender's next remark. There was none. The bartender made the drinks. Norbert carried them to a booth.

"Here's to life," he said, his tone sour.

"Are you troubled about something?" Nachman blurted out the question.

"That's how I seem to you?"

"Is there a problem?"

"Not my problem."

"Whose, then?"

"A guy in my department. You wouldn't understand."

"So it's an academic problem?"

"The most academic problem."

"What do you mean?"

"You heard of Plato? The ancient Greeks talked about this problem in their philosophy departments. It's about epistemology and fucking."

"Come on, Norbert, spare me the lecture. What about this guy in your department?"

Norbert shook his head, evidently overwhelmed by the prospect of telling Nachman about the guy. Muscles began working in Norbert's jaw, as if balls of feeling were being chewed. He seemed to have too much to say.

Nachman urged gently, "Tell me. What is the guy's problem?"

"I already told you too much. I shouldn't have said anything."

"You said almost nothing."

"All right, a student came on to him. That's the problem. O.K.?"

"Could you say a little more?"

"Forgive me for saying this, but you live a small life. Somebody gives you a pencil and a piece of paper and you are a happy Nachman. Like a kid on a beach. Give him a pail and he is king of the sand. You follow? The sand is like life, but all you need is a pail."

"Is this about me?"

"Of course not."

"But you sound angry. Are you angry?" Nachman asked, risking the worst possible answer. He couldn't go on with so much bad feeling suppressed.

"I'm angry at the guy with the problem. What a jerk. Imagine you are in your office, and a beautiful girl in a miniskirt is standing two inches from your nose. She is looking into your eyes and she smells good."

"Why is she standing two inches from your nose?"

"It isn't because she is nearsighted. She has no idea that anything she does has consequences. She is a girl."

"All right, go on."

"This girl is asking for advice about her major. Naturally, given such a provocative question, blood begins bulging in your manly part."

"So what did this guy do?"

"He told her to get the hell out of his office and phone in her question."

"I'm beginning to see the picture."

"You disapprove? This is a story about nature. To you, maybe, nature is a foreign language."

"Finish the story. What happened with the girl?"

"This guy kissed her and he put his hand between her legs."

"Just like that? What did she say?"

"She said 'Ohhhhhh.'"

"I see the picture."

"The guy can't eat. Can't sleep. He is crazy with jealousy because she sleep with other guys. Look, it's late. Do you want to get out of this dump and go home? You must want to go home. Say the word. Whatever you want."

"If it helps you to talk, Norbert, I'll listen all night. But there is something I must tell you."

"You needn't bother. I know you feel compromised. Adele told me about the mustache. She told me everything. It's not your fault that you saw her."

"So you're angry at Adele?"

"I love Adele. Who wouldn't love her? I asked her why is the mustache so important? Why do you need him? She says she doesn't know why. Nachman, you live with numbers. One plus one is two. It was always two, and it will always be two. For you there are problems, but no mysteries. The solutions exist, so take a vacation."

"Don't say another word. A vision is coming. I see a man who looks like me walking on a beach. He is on vacation. Now he is holding a shell to his ear, listening to the ocean, the chaos in which this shell was born. He knows that it was shaped according to a law which is expressed in the ratio of the rings on the shell. My God, he realizes, the shell can be described mathematically. The shell is a resolution of chaos, a mathematical entity. Do you understand?"

"Yes. You are constitutionally incapable of taking a vacation."

"What's real is numbers. When I solve a problem, I collect a piece of the real. Other men collect paintings, cars, Hawaiian shirts. They even collect women. So I'm a little different. You're angry at Adele, but why at me?"

"You need to believe I'm angry at you?"

Norbert was clearly angry at Nachman, but his anger was like the anger a parent feels for a much loved child. He was angry also because he had felt obliged, as a matter of pride, to confess the affair with the student. His confession had sounded like boasting. It was forced, somehow unconvincing. Nachman understood that Norbert was embarrassed as well as angry and that he was concerned to protect his wife.

"Does Adele know about the guy who kissed the girl?" Nachman asked.

"A man is a man."

"He doesn't have to account for himself?"

"There is always something for which there is no accounting. Take, for example, the whole world."

"This is between you and me, not you and the whole world. If you're angry at me, you should tell me why."

"Let's go. I'll drive you home." Norbert got up and strode to the bar. He reached into his pants pockets, fingers scrabbling along his thighs, searching for money to tip the bartender. There had been ugly tension between them when he ordered. The gesture, as Nachman understood it, meant that

Norbert was leaving with no hard feelings. It also meant that Norbert had forgiven Nachman.

They drove in silence to Nachman's house. As Nachman got out of the car, Norbert said, "Come to dinner this Friday. Adele told me to invite you." Norbert's expression, in the glow of the dashboard, was unreadable. His big head and the wide slope of his shoulders resembled a pit bull's. The shape was very familiar to Nachman. He realized that even if he saw only Norbert's head, at a distance, in a crowded street among a hundred moving heads, it would be enough for him to recognize his old friend. Nachman said, "I'll look forward to dinner."

Later that night, Nachman sat in bed reading. The book was called "Die Innenwelt der Mathematik." Nachman read German slowly and with difficulty, struggling with the sentences, consulting a dictionary every few minutes. Five pages took him nearly an hour, but he persisted. The book examined the question of whether mathematics was a social creation or a mysterious gift offered to certain individuals. Nachman didn't see how it could be a social creation. Mathematicians collaborated sometimes, but he had never heard anyone say, "We solved the problem." Nachman had never even met a mathematician who could tell you how a solution had come to him or her. It just came or it didn't. The great genius Ramanujan said that the goddess Namakkal came to him in his dreams bearing formulas. Well, no goddess had ever come to Nachman. But he did occasionally awake at night and stumble from his bed to a table where he kept a pencil and paper. In the morning, when he discovered that he had scribbled the solution to a problem, he didn't always remember having done so. What could be less social? It couldn't even be said that Nachman socialized with himself. In truth, he didn't really know what "social" meant. He and Norbert were the closest of friends, but were they social? Norbert was Norbert. In his pit-bull head, he dreamed of cars. Nachman was Nachman. He dreamed of numbers.

With the "Innenwelt" book open in his lap, Nachman fell asleep and had a vivid, frightening dream. He saw Adele kissing the mustache man. Nachman ran desperately toward them to pull her away. "No!" he cried, and he found himself awake, crying, "No, no, no!" his feet churning beneath the blanket, running nowhere.

Shaken by the dream, Nachman turned off the lamp and lay staring into the darkness. He didn't know what, if anything, his dream had revealed to him. He was aware only of tumultuous feeling. He'd been aware of it before, when Adele had asked if he was in love with her. He imagined the silent question in her green eyes, and he heard her say, "I thought we were friends." Nachman suddenly felt very lonely, lying in the darkness, wondering if he was in love with Adele.

# The Kiss

Isaac Babel

At the beginning of August, headquarters sent us to Budziatycze to regroup. The Poles had occupied it at the beginning of the war, but we had been quick to win it back. Our brigade entered the shetl at dawn, I arrived later in the day. The best billets had already been taken, and I ended up at the schoolmaster's house. He was a paralyzed old man sitting in an armchair in a low-ceilinged room, among buckets with fruit-bearing lemon trees. On his head was a Tyrolean hat with a feather. His gray beard lay on his chest, which was covered with cigarette ash. Babbling, his eyes fluttering, he seemed to be asking me for something. I washed, went to the headquarters, and didn't come back until night. My orderly, Mishka Surovtsev, a cunning Cossack from Orenburg, gave me a full report: besides the paralyzed old man, there was also a daughter present, Elizaveta Alekseyevna Tomilina, and her five-year-old son who was also called Mishka, like Surovtsev. The daughter, the widow of an officer who had fallen in the Great War, was a respectable woman but, according to Surovtsev's information, would be willing to make herself available to a proper gentleman.

"I can arrange things," he told me, and went off to the kitchen, where he began clattering about with plates. The schoolmaster's daughter helped him. As they cooked, Surovtsev told her of my brave feats, how I knocked two Polish officers out of their saddles in a battle, and how much the Soviet authorities respected me. He was answered by the restrained, soft voice of Tomilina.

"Where d'you sleep?" Surovtsev asked her as he left the kitchen. "You should come sleep closer to us, we're living, breathing people."

He brought me some fried eggs in a gigantic frying pan, and put it on the table.

"She's up for it," he said, sitting down. "She just hasn't come out and said it yet."

At that very instant we heard whispering, rattling, and heavy, careful steps. We didn't have time to finish eating our war meal, when some old men on crutches and old women with kerchiefs on their heads came hobbling through the house. They dragged little Mishka's bed into the dining room, into the lemon-tree forest, next to his grandfather's armchair. The feeble guests, readying themselves to defend Elizaveta Alekseyevna's honor, huddled together in a flock, like sheep in a storm, and, barricading the door, spent the whole night silently playing cards, whispering, "My trick," and falling silent at every sound. I was so mortified, so embarrassed, that I simply could not fall asleep behind that door, and could barely wait for the sun to rise.

"For your information," I told Tomilina when I ran into her in the hall, "for your information, I have a law degree and am a member of the so-called intelligentsia!"

Rigid, her arms dangling, she stood there in her old-fashioned housedress which clung tightly to her slim body. Without blinking, she looked straight at me with widening blue eyes sparkling with tears.

Within two days we were friends. The schoolmaster's family, a family of kind, weak people, lived in boundless fear and uncertainty. Polish officials had convinced them that Russia had fallen in fire and barbarity, like Rome. They were overcome with a childlike, fearful joy when I told them of Lenin, the Moscow Arts Theater, of a Moscow in which the future was raging. In the evenings, twenty-two-year-old Bolshevik generals with scraggly red beards came to visit us. We smoked Moscow cigarettes, we ate meals that Elizaveta Alekseyevna prepared with army provisions, and sang student songs. Leaning forward in his armchair, the paralyzed old man listened avidly, his Tyrolean hat bobbing to the rhythm of our songs. Through all these days the old man was in the clutches of a sudden, stormy, vague hope, and, in order not to let anything darken his happiness, he did his best to overlook the foppish bloodthirstiness and loudmouthed simplicity with which in those days we solved all the problems of the world.

After our victory over the Poles—the family counsel decided—the Tomilins would move to Moscow. We would have a celebrated professor cure the old man, Elizaveta Alekseyevna would take classes, and we would put Mishka in the selfsame school that his mother had once gone to at Patriarkhy Prudy. The future seemed incontestably ours, and war was merely a stormy prelude to happiness, happiness, the core of our being. The only things that remained unresolved were the specific details, and nights passed in discussing these details, mighty nights, in which the candle end was mirrored in the dull bottle of our homebrewed vodka. Elizaveta Alekseyevna, blossoming, was our silent listener. I have never met a more impulsive, free, or timorous being. In the evenings, cunning Surovtsev, in the wicker cart he had requisitioned back in Kuban, drove us up the hill to where the abandoned house of the Counts Gasiorowski shone in the flames of the sunset. The horses, thin but long-bodied and thoroughbred, were running in step in their red reins. A carefree earring swayed on Surovtsev's ear. Round towers rose up from a pit that was overgrown with a yellow tablecloth of flowers. The ruined walls drew a crooked line flooded with ruby-red blood across the sky. A dog-rose bush hid its berries, and blue steps, the remains the flight of stairs that Polish kings had once mounted, shone in the thickets. Once, as I sat there, I pulled Elizaveta Alekseyevna's head toward me and kissed her. She slowly pulled away, got up, and leaned against the wall, holding on to it with both hands. She stood there motionless, and around her, around her dazzled head, swirled a fiery, dusty ray. Shuddering, as if she had just heard something, Tomilina raised her head and let go of the wall. She ran down the hill, her uncertain steps becoming faster. I called out to her, she didn't answer. Below, red-cheeked Surovtsev lay sprawled out in his wicker cart.

At night, when everyone was asleep, I crept to Elizaveta Alekseyevna's room. She sat reading, holding her book at arm's length. Her hand, lying on the table, seemed lifeless. She turned when I knocked, and rose.

"No," she said, looking me in the eyes, "please, dearest, no." And embracing my head with her long, bare arms, she gave me an increasingly violent, never-ending, silent kiss.

The shrill ring of the telephone in the next room pushed us apart. An orderly was calling from headquarters.

"We're pulling out!" he said over the phone. "You are to report to the brigade commander now!"

I rushed out of the house without even putting on my hat, stuffing my papers into my bag as I ran. Horses were being brought out of yards, horsemen galloped yelling through the darkness. The brigade commander, tying his cloak, told us that the Poles had broken through our lines near Lublin, and that we had been ordered to execute a bypass maneuver. Both regiments pulled out an hour later. The old man, awoken from his sleep, anxiously followed me with his eyes through the leaves of a lemon tree.

"Promise me you will return," he kept saying, his head wagging.

Elizaveta Alekseyevna, a fur jacket over her batiste night-dress, accompanied us out onto the street. An invisible squadron raced past violently. At the curve in the road by the field I turned to look back—Elizaveta Alekseyevna was bending down to fix the jacket of little Mishka, who was standing in front of her, and the erratic light of the lamp burning on the windowsill streamed over the tender bones of her nape.

After riding a hundred kilometers without rest, we joined forces with the Fourteenth Cavalry Division and, fighting, we began our retreat. We slept in our saddles. At rest stops, we fell to the ground overwhelmed with exhaustion, and our horses, pulling at their reins, dragged us fast asleep through the harvested fields. It was the beginning of autumn and the soundless drizzling Galician rain. Huddled together in a bristling silent herd, we dodged and circled, fell into the Poles' waiting net, but managed to slip out again just before they could close it. We lost all sense of time. When we were quartered in the church in Toscza, it did not even occur to me that we were only nine versts from Budziatycze. Surovtsev reminded me, we exchanged glances.

"The problem is that the horses are exhausted," he said cheerfully. "Otherwise we could go."

"We couldn't anyway," I replied. "They'd notice if we left in the middle of the night."

And we went. We tied gifts to our saddles—a clump of sugar, a fox-fur wrap, and a live, two-week-old goat kid. The road went through a swaying wet forest, a metallic star strayed through the crowns of the oaks. In less than an hour we arrived at the shtetl, its burned-out center filled with trucks, pale with flour dust, and with machine-gun-cart harnesses and broken shafts. Without dismounting, I knocked on the familiar window. A white cloud flitted through the room. Wearing the same batiste nightdress with its hanging lace, Tomilina came rushing out onto the porch. She took my hand in her hot hand and led me into the house. Men's underclothes were hanging out to dry on the broken branches of the lemon trees, and unknown men were sleeping in camp beds lined up in tight rows like in a field hospital. With crooked, hardened mouths they yelled out hoarsely in their sleep, breathing greedily and loud, their dirty feet jutting out. The house was occupied by our War Spoils Commission, and the Tomilins had been bundled off into a single room.

"When will you take us away from here?" Elizaveta Alekseyevna asked, clasping my hand.

The old man woke, his head wagging. Little Mishka cuddled the goat kid, and brimmed over with happy, soundless laughter. Above him stood Surovtsev, puffing himself up. Out of the pockets of his Cossack trousers he shook spurs, shot-through coins, and a whistle hanging on a yellow string. In this house occupied by the War Spoils Commission there was nowhere to hide, and Tomilina and I went to the wooden shed where the potatoes and beehive frames were kept in winter. There, in the shed, I saw what an inevitably pernicious path that kiss had been, the path that had begun by the castle of the Counts Gasiorowski. Surovtsev came knocking shortly before dawn.

"When will you take us from here?" Elizaveta Alekseyevna asked, turning her head away.

I stood there silently, and then walked over to the house to say good-bye to the old man.

"The problem is we're running out of time," Surovtsev said, blocking my way. "Get on your horse, we've got to go!"

He jostled me out onto the street and brought me my horse. Elizaveta Alekseyevna gave me her chilled hand. As always, she held her head high. The horses, well rested overnight, carried us off at a brisk trot. The flaming sun rose through the black tangle of the oak trees. The rejoicing morning filled my whole being.

A glade in the forest opened up before us. I directed my horse toward it, and, turning back to Surovtsev, called out to him, "We could have stayed a bit longer. You came for me too early!"

"Too early?" he said, riding up closer to me, pushing away the wet branches that dropped their sparkling raindrops. "If it wasn't for the old man, I'd have come for you even earlier. He was trying to tell me something and suddenly was all nerves, started squawking, and keeled over. I rush to him, I look, he's dead, dead as a doornail!"

The forest came to an end. We rode over a plowed field without paths. Standing up in his stirrups, looking all around, whistling, Surovtsev sniffed out the right direction and, breathing it in with the air, hunched forward and went galloping toward it.

We arrived in time. The men of the squadron were just being awakened. The sun shone warmly, promising a hot day. That morning our brigade crossed the former border of the Kingdom of Poland.

# Maria de Covina

## Dagoberto Gilb

I've got two sports coats, about six ties, three dressy pants, Florsheims I polish *a la madre*, and three weeks ago I bought a suit, with silk lining, at Lemonde for Men. It came with a matching vest. That's what made it for me. I love getting all duded up, looking fine, I really do. This is the thing: I like women. No, wait. I *love* women. I know that don't sound like anything new, nothing every guy wouldn't tell you. I mean it though, and it's that I can't say so better. It's not like I do anything different when I'm around them. I'm not like aggressive, going after them, hustling. I don't play that. I don't do anything except have a weakness for them. I don't ask anybody out. I already have my girlfriend Diana. Still, it's like I feel drunk around them. Like they make me so *pedo* I can't move away. See what I'm saying? So yeah, of course I love working nights at The Broadway.

Women's perfume is everywhere, and I'm dizzy while I'm there.

Even if what I'm about to say might not sound right, I'm saying it: It's not just me, it's them too, it's them *back*, maybe even first. Okay, I realize this sounds bad, so I won't talk about it. But why else did they put me in the Gifts department? I didn't know *ni nada* about that stuff, and I noticed right away that most customers were women. And I'm not meaning to brag, but the truth is I sell, they buy. They're older women almost always, rich I see now, because the things we have on the racks—*cositas como* vases and statues and baskets and bowls, from Russia, Germany, Africa, Denmark, France, Argentina, everywhere—are originals and they're expensive. These ladies, maybe they're older, but a lot really look good for being older, they come in and they ask my opinion. They're smiling when they ask me what I'd like if it was for me. I try to be honest. I smile a lot. I smile because I'm happy.

You know what? Even if I'm wrong, *no le bace*, I don't care. Because when I go down the escalator, right at the bottom is Cindy in Cosmetics. She says, "Is your mommy coming for you tonight?" Cindy's almost blond, very pretty, and way out there. She leans over the glass to get close to me. She wears her blouses a little low-cut. She's big for being such a *flaquita*.

"Maybe," I say. "Maybe not."

"Don't marry her yet." That bedroom voice of hers.

"What difference will it make?"

"None to me," she says.

"You talk big," I say, "but do you walk the walk?"

"You know where I am. What're we waiting for?"

She's not wrong. I'm the one who only talks the talk. I don't lie to myself. For instance, I'm about to be nineteen, but I pretend I'm twenty. I do get away with it. I pass for older. I'm not sure why that's true—since I'm thirteen I've had a job—or why I want it to be. I feel older when I say I am. For the same reason I let them think I know so much about sex. *Ya sabes*, pretend that I'm all experienced, like I'm all bad. Lots of girls, and that I know what they like. I feel like it's true when I'm around them. It's what Cindy thinks. And I want her to, I like it that she does, but at the same time it makes me scared of her. She's not pretending, and I'm afraid she'll find out about me: The truth is that my only experience is with Diana. I'm too embarrassed to admit it, and I don't, even to her.

It's not just Cindy though, and this isn't talk, and though it might sound like it, honest, I'm not trying to brag. Over in Women's Fashions is Ana, a *morena* with green eyes, and strong, pretty legs. She's shy. Not that shy. She wants to be in love, wants a wedding, wants a baby. In Housewares is Brigit. Brigit is Russian, and sometimes she's hard to understand. You should see her. She's got the bones of a black girl, but her skin is snow. I think she's older than she looks. She'll go out with me, I know it. I don't know how she'd be, and I wonder. Over there, down the mall, at Lemonde for Men, is where Liz works. That's who I bought my suit from. Liz is fun. Likes to laugh. The Saturday. I picked up my suit we had lunch together, and then one night, when I knew she was working, just before we closed, I called her. I told her I was hungry and would she want to go somewhere after. She said yeah. We only kissed good-bye. The next time she was letting me feel her. She likes it, and she's not embarrassed that she does. I think about her a lot. Touching her. But I don't want this to sound so *gacho*, porno or something. I like her, that's what I mean. I like everything about her. I don't know how to say it better.

"You're such a liar," Maria says. She's my boss. The assistant manager of Gifts and Luggage, Silverware and China. I worry that she knows how old I really am, and she's going by that. Or that she knows I'm not really going to college in the day. I don't know why I can't be honest about having that other job. I work for A-Tron Monday through Friday. A shipping clerk. It's a good job too. But it's better to say you're studying for something better. I am going to go to college next year, after I save some money.

"What're you saying?"

"You just want to get them," Maria de Covina says. "You're no different than any other man."

I have told her a lot, I'm not sure why. Probably because she catches me all the time talking to them. The first times I thought she was getting mad and going around checking up on me because I'd be on a break and taking too long. But she's cool. We just seemed to run into each other a lot, and she would like shake her head at me, so now I tell her how I'm thinking. I told her about Liz after she saw us on that first Saturday, eating lunch in the mall.

"It's not true," I say.

"It's not *true*," she whines. She often repeats what I say in a mocking voice. Sometimes she gets close to me, and this time she gets real close, close enough to reach her hand around and grab one of my *nalgas*. "It's not *true*."

"Watch it, Covina," I say. "You Italians think everything you squeeze is a soft *tomate*, but Mexicans got *chiles* that burn."

I call her Maria de Covina because she lives in West Covina and drives in. I call her Italian because she doesn't know a word of Spanish, and Italians can be named Maria. I can't let up. She really is Mexican American, just the spoiled, *pocha* princess type. But I don't let on. She tells me her last name over and over. What do you think Mata is? she asks. Does *Mata* sound Italian to you? I say maybe, yeah. Like a first name like Maria, I say. Like a last name like Corona. Probably it's that, I tell her, and you're messing with me. I don't understand yet what you're up to. Why is it you want everyone to think you're a Mexican when you're not? In my family, everybody always wished they weren't. So she calls me names and means them because this really upsets her. Stupid, she calls me. Buttbreath. Say those in Spanish, I suggest to her, and we'll see what you know. She says, *Estúpido*. One wrong, I tell her. What about the other? No reply. You don't know, do you? Not a clue, right? This is a game we play, and though there is part of me that can't believe she takes it seriously, another part sees how my teasing bothers her too much.

"Besides, no Chicanos live in West Covina."

"Yes they do."

It cracks me up how serious she sounds. She's too easy. "I never met any from there, ever. It's probably too rich or something."

"You've never even been there, and I bet you don't even know where it is."

"Me and nobody like me."

"My parents just never taught me any Spanish."

"Did they talk it at home?"

"Not really."

"You see? What'd I tell you?"

"Asshole." She whispers that in my ear because we're on the floor and customers are around.

"When they were talking something, if they did, it probably was Italian and you didn't even know it."

I never tell my girlfriend Diana anything about these other girls. Though she's been mad at me anyway. We used to go out more often than we do now, but with my two jobs, and her school, it's almost only been weekends. After we go to a movie, we head back to her place because her parents go to sleep so early. I take her to the door and we kiss and then I leave. I park on the busy street around the corner and I walk back and crawl through her window. It's a big bedroom because she used to share with her sister, who went away to be a nurse. She's very sheltered in a certain way, in that Catholic way, but I'm not Diana's first boyfriend, though I am the first one she's made love to. She let me the second time we went out because she thought I expected it. Because I was so experienced. She's sixteen. She doesn't look it, but she acts it. She worries. She's scared of everything she likes. The first time she orgasmed, she told me a couple of months ago, she didn't really know what it was, and it felt too good, so she called her sister's best friend, who can talk about any subject and especially sex, and asked if she was all right.

She'll let me do certain things to her, and now she'll be on top sometimes. But she worries that one of us will get too loud. She has been a couple of times. I feel her pulsate in there real hard. She worries that we'll fall asleep after and her mom or dad will be up before we know it. That happened once, and I got out of there, but she's been really worried ever since about everything, every little noise, like they're listening.

The only thing in the room that isn't just for a girl is a statue I gave her of *The Thinker*. It came from Gifts. It had a chip in the wood base and was being sold at 20 percent discount. I kept looking at it, trying to decide if I should buy it. It's big, heavy. He looks smart. I imagined having it in my own place when I got one. I guess that Maria and Joan, the manager of our department, saw how often I stared at it, and so one day they gave it to me, all gift wrapped, a ribbon and bow. I was surprised, embarrassed even, that they bought me a present, and one so expensive, and I didn't think I should accept it, until they explained how it only cost a dollar—they'd marked it down as damaged and, being the manager and assistant manager, signed off on it. This was one of those nights that Diana came to the store to pick me up after work. She was suspicious of Maria, which seemed crazy to me since she was twenty-six and my boss, and then, as we were going down the escalator, of Cindy, who made a sexy wink at me, which didn't seem crazy. So right there in the parking lot I gave *The Thinker* to Diana, and it's been on her bedstand since.

"They got these pretty, glass flowers," I say, "and I keep thinking of ways to get them for you. You know, cheap."

"They're not for me," she says. "Those are gifts for grand-mothers or mothers."

"Well, then I could give them to your mom."

"A gift from you would be a good idea."

I'm not sure I want that yet. "I could give them to my mom, too. You know, for Mother's Day."

"You better not," she says. "It's stealing."

"Joan sells marked-down things all the time."

"I think you should stop thinking like this."

"But it's easy," I tell her. "I'm good at it."

"How do you know if you're good at it?"

"I know what I'm good at."

"You know I don't like that kind of talk."

"You *know* I don't *like* that kind of *talk*." Lately I've been im-itating Maria de Covina.

"You better go," she says.

"Would you stop it," I say. "I'm playing, I'm only teasing."

"You really should go anyway," she says. She's naked, looking for her underwear in the bedsheets, in the dark. "I'm afraid. We're taking too many chances."

I don't take too many chances. One time I did sell something to a friend, for example, for a much lower price than was on the tag. But that was instead of, say, just giving it to him in the bag when he buys something else for a normal price. Which is stealing. I wouldn't do that. Another way is, a customer comes and buys an item, but instead of making a normal receipt, I ring it out on our long form, the one in three-colored triplicate, that one we use when the item has to be delivered. I wait for an expensive purchase. I give the customer the white copy, put the green copy in the register, then fill out the pink copy later-in blue pencil so it looks right, like it's from the stencil. I can stick whatever I want in a box, put that pink copy with a name and address on it, and mail it out of the store. The truth is I think of everything and do nothing. It's only a little game I play in my mind. There's nothing here I want. Well, one time I wanted a ship, a pirate ship to me, with masts and sails and rope the width of string. It was going off the floor because it never sold in over a year, and some items like this are smashed up and thrown away instead of sent back—written off as a loss. I thought I should just take it home instead of destroying it, but Maria insisted on writing me out a slip and selling it to me for three dollars. I gave it to my mom.

"If you really want the valise," I tell Mrs. Huffy, "I'll sell it to you marked down as damaged." Mrs. Huffy sells the luggage. She and I often work the same shift. Sometimes she comes over and sells gifts, and sometimes I sell luggage, but mostly we keep to our separate areas. Maria takes care of the silverware and china. The valise that Mrs. Huffy likes is going to be ripped up and trashed because it's not made anymore and can't be returned to the supplier for a refund.

"It seems like such a waste to throw it away." Mrs. Huffy fidgets with her glasses all the time. She has a chain on them so she doesn't put them down and forget them. You can't tell most of the time if she sees better with them off or with them on. Sometimes the glasses go nervously onto the top of her hair, which is silver gray, the same color as the chain and the frames.

"It is a waste if you ask me."

"You'd think they'd call the Salvation Army instead." Glasses hanging like a necklace.

Mrs. Huffy makes me think of what Diana will be like when she's old. Still worried. "But they're not. They're throwing it away."

"It's terrible," she says.

"I could just sell it to you."

She takes the glasses up to her nose and stares at me. "You can't do that. I wouldn't. Security looks at the receipt." When we leave the building at night, guards examine our belongings, and if we've bought anything from the store, they check the receipt to make sure it matches.

"We'll get it marked down. I'll ask Maria." Everything's okay if a manager or assistant manager says so.

"It wouldn't be right." Glasses on the head.

"Okay then, but I think it's no big deal."

"Do you think she'd do it?"

"I'm sure she would."

"I can't." Glasses on the nose. Holding the valise, snapping it open, snapping it closed. "I can't ask."

"I told you already I'd ask. I know she won't care."

"I don't know."

"*Conzo quieras*, whatever you decide." I'm walking back to Gifts because I see a customer.

"I don't know," Mrs. Huffy says. "Are you sure Maria would?"

Maria saw me the other night in the parking lot with Cindy, and she wouldn't stop asking me about it. So? she'd say, so? I didn't think I should talk about it. Come on, did you get some or not? I didn't think it was right to talk about it. But she kept insisting and, finally, it seemed okay. I told her how Cindy and I were parked near each other and she said something about a good-night kiss. She started pressing against me hard, and I just put my hand on a *chiche* and then she wrapped her leg around me even harder and rubbed up against me until she put her hand on me. She was physically hot, like sweating. She put her hand down there, I put my hand down there, and then we went into her car. I didn't want to tell Covina the rest, I didn't think I should. But still she says, So? Whadaya mean, *so*? I'm delaying because I feel her close behind me, and I'm not sure.

Did you or not? she says. The store's just closed, and I'm at my register, clearing it while we're talking, about to take my tray out to count money, and she's behind me very close. Why don't you want to tell me? she says. She's got her *chiches* against me, moving just a little, and, I don't know, I don't mind but I'm embarrassed too. In case someone sees. But I don't say anything. I'm also surprised. I don't know why it hadn't crossed my mind. She had her register to clear, and she left.

"I don't like it." Diana's worrying. She's in pajamas.

"It's no big deal," I say. We're whispering to each other in the dark. I'm not sure why it's so dark this night but it is. I surprised her when I came to the window. I had to say her name a few times to wake her up.

"You better stop," she says. Even though I can't see them, the glass flowers I bought damaged are in a vase next to *The Thinker*. I told her I didn't want them for either her mom or mine, and once she saw them, how beautiful they were, she wanted them. "You're gonna get *caught*."

"You're gonna get *caught*," I say.

"Why would Maria be doing this?" she asks. "I don't trust her."

I feel like Diana is really sensing Cindy, or Liz. I told her I had to work Saturday night, and that's why we couldn't go out. I feel like it's because I'm talking too much about all this to Covina, and it's in the air, that I'm not being smart, talking *esas cosas* out loud. "Come on, it's crazy," I tell Diana. "She's a lot older than me, and she's the assistant manager of the department. She knows what she's doing."

Suddenly she starts crying.

"What's the matter?" I ask.

She's sobbing into her pillow.

"You're making too much noise," I'm whispering. "You're gonna wake up your parents."

"You have to go," she says. She's talking in a normal voice, which is really loud at this time of night. Her face is all wet. I try to kiss her, but she pushes me away. "You have to go," she says.

"Can't we make love?" I'm being quiet at the open window, and though my eyes have adjusted, it's so dark, and I can barely see her in the bed. "Don't you want to make love?"

I feel sick. I love women, but I realize I don't want to lose Diana. I love her.

Covina shakes her head as I tell her how Diana was acting. Mexican men, she says.

I do like it that she thinks of me as a man. I like being a man, even if it makes me feel too old for Diana. It's confusing. I'm not sure what to do. I wonder if she'd say the same if she didn't think I was almost twenty-one.

I go to the stockroom, and I sit on the edge of the gray desk. "Mrs. Huffy wants this valise real bad. You think you could sign this?" I've already made out a receipt. Instead of forty-five dollars, I made it for forty-five cents, damaged.

Covina gets up, and without kissing me, *ni nada*, she pushes her breast into my face. She has one hand under it, and another on my neck. Pretty quick she opens her blouse and she pulls up her bra and we're both excited and she reaches over and slams the stockroom door and she gets on her knees between mine. I wouldn't tell her, but nobody's ever done that to me before. It was exciting, and I was scared—it *was* right there in our stockroom—and I guess I am a little shocked too, but I don't want her to know it. You know. I follow her to her apartment because she told me to. Before I didn't even think about whether she had her own apartment. I didn't really want to go. And I didn't do very well. She probably saw how inexperienced I am really, and then I made the mistake of telling her how I'm in love with Diana, and how bad I'm feeling.

So I'm tired when I clock in because I stayed with her. I was late in the morning getting to A-Tron, and I wouldn't have gone in if I already didn't know there were a lot of orders we had to fill. Mrs. Huffy is already in Silverware and China when I get to the floor, so worried she can't even take her glasses off when she sees me, and Joan stops me in the middle of Gifts. Joan never works at night.

When Mrs. Huffy checked out with the valise, a security guard opened her package, and asked for the receipt, and the guard said he was going to keep it and make sure it was on the up and up the next day. Instead of, like, scratching the valise when she got home so it really did look damaged, instead of waiting for Joan to deal with it so she could tell us to never do anything like this again, Mrs. Huffy panicked and brought the valise back in the morning.

"Ms. Mata told me everything," Stemp says. Stemp works

for the LAPD, or used to, or something like that. I already know who he is, but I'd never talked to him before. He never talks to anybody. He might be chief of security at The Broadway. He wears cheap black slacks and a cheap white shirt and a cheap, plain blue tie. He looks like he might rock in his swivel chair, but he doesn't. He just has it tilted back, his hands folded onto his *panza*. The office has no decorations, no photos or paintings or mirrors on the walls. On his gray desk is the cheapest lamp they sell in Furniture, which is across from Gifts, and one of those heavy black phones. He has a sheet of paper and a pen in front of him. "She told me about how you used triplicate forms and used our courtesy mailing service and how you sold goods to your friends." He stares at me for a very long time, satisfied like he just ate a big meal.

"I never did anything like that," I say. I couldn't believe Maria told him my ideas. "It's not true," I say.

"It's not true," he repeats. He shakes his head with only his eyes. "Do you realize that Ms. Mata was building a career here?"

"She didn't do anything. I know she never did anything."

He really shakes his head. "I don't have time for this. I already have it all." He slides the paper over to me. "Just sign it and get outta here."

I read his form. It lists all these ways I took things from the store, and how Maria cooperated.

"No," I say. "Maria didn't cooperate, she didn't do anything. I didn't do anything either."

"I can call the police right now if you'd prefer. We can deal with this in that manner."

"I guess. I have to think."

He sends me off after I sign a form admitting that I sold a forty-five-dollar valise to Mrs. Huffy for forty-five cents. I loved this job so much. I really loved being here at The Broadway, and I can't think of what I'll do now. I head to the parking lot, and I'm in my car, and I'm trying to decide whether I should go over to Diana's or to Maria's, if either of them would want to see me, when I see Liz waving at me. I get out of the car. How come you haven't called me? she wants to know. I'm wearing the suit I bought from her store. The vest is buttoned but the jacket isn't. I do always feel good in it.

# Behind the Heart

**Djuna Barnes**

"**N**ow it is of a little boy that I would tell you, Madame, and what he meant for just one week to a lady who had great consequence because her spirit had been level always, in spite of the cost, and for her it had been much, for she at forty had known life for almost forty years, which is not so with most people, n'est-ce pas, Madame? Twenty years are given to a child in the beginning on which to grow, and not to be very wise about sadness or happiness, so that the child can wander about a little, and look into the sky and at the ground, and wonder what is to be that has not yet any being, that he may come upon his fate with twenty years to find safety in. And I think with the boy it was this way, but with her it was different, her life was a fate with her always, and she was walking with it when she and the boy met.

"Truly, Madame, seldom in the world is it that I talk of boys, therefore you must know that this was a boy who was very special. He was very young, Madame, scarcely twenty, and I think he had lived only a little while, a year perhaps, perhaps two. He was a Southerner, so that what was bright and quick in him, often seemed strange, so bound about he was with quiet. And she, Madame, she was a Northerner, and introspection hurried her. It was in Paris, Madame, and in the autumn and in the time of rain. For weeks, days and nights for weeks it had been raining. It was raining under the trees, and on the Avenues, and over the houses and along the Seine, so that the water seemed too wet; and the buttresses of churches and the eaves of buildings were weeping steadily; clinging to the angles, endlessly sliding down went the rain. People sat in cafés with their coat collars up, for with the rain the cold came; and everyone was talking everywhere about danger in the weather and in some cafés there was talk of politics and rain, and love and rain, and rain and ruined crops, and in one café a few people talked of Hess, this lady, Madame, of whom I am speaking. And they said that it was a shame that Hess, who had come to Paris again for the first time in two years to rest and to look over her house and to be a little gay, should have, in her third week, to be taken ill.

"And it was true. Scarcely three weeks, and she was hurried under the knife, so that all her friends were very sorry as they drank. And some said she was very brave, and some said she was beautiful, and some that she was alone always, and some said she was dour, and that, in an amusing way, she took the joy out of life with her laugh. And some of them wondered if it would be necessary to forget her.

"And they went to see her, and one of them came with the boy, that was on the day that she was to go home, and she was not very strong yet, and she looked at the boy, and she put her hand out to him and she said: 'You will come and you will stay with me until it is time.' And he said, 'I will come.'

"And that is how it was, Madame, that she came upon her week that was without fate as we understand it, and that is why I am telling it.

"Do I know, Madame, what it was about him that she liked? It was perhaps what anyone looking at him would have seen and liked, according to their nature. That was a curious thing about him, people who did not like him were not the right people; a sort of test he seemed to be of something in people that they had mislaid and would be glad to have again.

"He had light long legs, and he walked straight forward, straight like an Indian his feet went, his body held back. And it was touching and ridiculous because it was the walk of a father of a family in the child of the father, a structural miscalculation dismissed when he sat down, for when he sat down he was a child without a father, from his little behind up he was so small. His hands were long and thin, and when he held her hands they were very frail, as if he would not use them long, but when he said *à bientôt* to his friends, Madame, his grip was strong and certain. But his smile, Madame, that was the gentlest thing about him. His teeth were even and white, but it wasn't so much the teeth that mattered, it was the mouth: The upper lip was a lip on a lip, a slight inner line making it double, like the smile of animals when it is spring; and where most mouths follow the line of the bone, his ran outward and upward, regardless of the skull.

"His chin was long and oval, and his eyes were like her eyes, as if they were kinspeople, brother and sister, but some happening apart. His were soft, and shining and eager, and hers were gentle and humorous and satiric. Sometimes he rolled his eyes up, so that one wondered if he were doing it on purpose, or if something in him was trying to think of something, and at that moment they would come back again without the thought, smiling and gentle.

"She lay on her great white bed with many lace pillows and pillows of holy embroidery behind her, and I think, Madame, she was very happy and taken aback, for she had known many loves; love of men who were grim and foolish and confident; love of men who were wise and conceited and nice; and men who knew only what they wanted. Now she looked at a boy and knew that she loved him with a love from back of the heart, alien and strange.

"He sat beside her, chin on hand, looking at her long, and she knew what was between them would be as he wished.

"And they talked about many things. She tried to tell him about her life, but what was terrible and ugly and painful she made funny for his sake; made legend, and folk-lore, and story, made it *largo* with the sleep in her voice, because he could not know it. And he told her of himself, quickly, as if it were a dream that he was forgetting and must hurry with. And he said: 'You like to think of death, and I don't like to think of death, because I saw it once and could not cry!' And she said: 'Do I know why you could not cry?' And he said, 'You know.'

"Then one night he said, 'I love you,' and she turned about, 'And do you love me,' she said, and he came beside her and knelt down and put his hands on either cheek, his mouth on her mouth, softly, swiftly, with one forward movement of the tongue, like an animal who is eager and yet afraid of a new grass, and he got up quickly. She noticed then that his eyes lay in the side of his head, not as human eyes that are lost in pro-file, but as the eyes of beasts, standing out clear, bossy and blue, the lashes slanting straight, even and down.

"And then, Madame, she said, 'How do you love me?' And he said, 'I love you more than anyone, as I love sister and mother and someone else I loved once and who is gone.' And happiness went marching with a guard of consternation. 'Mother,' he said, 'is beautiful and thin, and though she is quiet, there is something in her she keeps speaking to: Hush, hush! for sister and me. Sister is beautiful and dark, and she sings deep down in her throat "Now I Lay Down My Heavy Load," with her head held back, like that, to find where it is to sing. And when she laughs, she laughs very hard, she has to sit down wherever she is for the laughter in her stomach, and she dances like mad, and when you are well we will dance together.'

"And then she said, 'Do you love me as a lover loves.' And he looked at her with those luminous apprehensive eyes, and went past her and he said, 'What you wish is yours.' And the moment she was happy, he leaned forward and said, 'Are you happy?,' and she said 'Yes,' and she was very nearly crying, 'And are you happy?,' she said to him, and he said, 'Frighteningly happy.' And then she said, 'Come and sit beside me,' and he came, then she began: 'Now where is that little boy I reached out my hand to and said, you will come with me and you will stay with me until it is time.' His eyes were wide with a kind of shadow of light. Her voice was far away, coming from a great distance to him. 'We lose that other one,' she said. 'When we come to know each other it is that way always, one comes and the other one goes away, one we lose for one we cannot find. Where is that other little boy? He's gone now and lost now——' His eyes were still looking at her with the shadow of light in them, and then suddenly he was laughing and crying all at once, with his eyes wide open, and his shoulders raised and leaning sideways, and she sat up toward him and put her arms around him as if it must be quick, and she said, 'My sweet! My sweet!,' and he was laughing and crying and saying, 'Always I must remember that I believed you.' And his hands between his legs pushed hard against the bed, and they knew that she had reminded them of something.

"The next morning she came to his bed where he slept, for

he slept many long hours like a child, and she lay down beside him and put her arms over his head on the pillow and leaned to waken him, and his mouth, closed in sleep, opened, and her teeth touched his teeth, and suddenly he drew his legs up and turned sideways and said, 'I dreamed of you all night, and before I dreamed, I lay here and I was you. My head was your head and my body was your body, and way down my legs were your legs, and on the left foot was your bracelet. I thought I was mad,' And he said, 'What is it that you are doing to me?' And she got up and went to the window, and she said, 'It is you who are doing it.'

"And presently he came in, in a long dressing gown, his eyes full of sleep, carrying the tray with the tea pot and the *brioches* and the pot of honey, and full of sleep he put crumbs and tea in his mouth, holding one of her hands with his hand. So, Madame, to still the pain at her heart she began making up a story and a plan that would never be.

'You are my little Groom,' she said, 'and we will go driving in the *Bois*, for that is certainly a thing one must do when one is in love, and you shall wear the long military cape, and we will drink cocktails at the Ritz bar, and we will go down the Seine in a boat, and then we will go to Vienna together, and we will drive through the city in an open carriage, and I shall hold your hand and we shall be very happy. And we will go down to Budapest by water, and you will wrap your cloak about you and everyone will think we are very handsome and mysterious, and you will know you have a friend.

"His eyes were enormous and his mouth smiled with the smaller inner smile, and he said, 'How could I have known that I was to be married!'

"And later, Madame, when she could get up and really walk, they wandered in the Luxembourg gardens, and he held her arm, and she showed him the statue of the queen, holding a little queen in her hand, and he showed her one of three boys running; and they looked at all the flowers beaten down by the rain and at the trellises of grapes and pears, that, covered in paper bags, looked in the distance like unknown lilies. Walking under the high, dark trees, with no branches until they were way up, he said, 'How much of you is mine?,' and she answered, 'All that you wish.' And he said, 'I should like to be with you at Christmas,' and he said, 'Mine and nobody else's?' And she said, 'Yours is nobody else's.'

"And then they went back home, Madame, and they had tea by a bright fire, and he said, 'You do not hurt anymore, and I must go now.' And she knew that there was a magic in them that would be broken when he went out of the house. And she said, 'What will you do when I die.'

"And he said, 'One word beneath the name.'

"And she said, 'What word?'

"And he said, 'Lover.'

"And then he began preparing to go away. Watching him dress, her heart dropped down, endlessly down, dark down it went, and joy put out a hand to catch it, and it went on falling; and sorrow put out a hand, and falling, it went falling down as he brushed his hair, and powdered his neck so slow, so delicate, turning his head this way and that, and over his shoulder looking at her, and away slowly, and back again quickly, looking at her, his eyes looking at her softly and gently.

"And it had begun to rain again and it was dark all about the candle he brought to his packing, his books and his shirts and his handkerchiefs and he was hurrying with the lock on his valise because a friend was coming to help him carry it, and his hair fell forward, long and straight and swinging, and he said, 'I will come back in ten days, and we will go. And now I will write to you every day.' And she said, 'You do not have to go,' and he answered her in his little light voice, 'I am going now so I will know what it will be like when you go away forever.' And she was trembling in the dark, and she went away into the bedroom, and stood with her back to the wall, a crying tall figure in the dark, crying and standing still, and he seemed to know it though she made no sound, for he came in to her and he put his hands on her shoulders, the thin forearms against her breast, and he said, 'You are deeply good, and is everything well with you?' And she said, 'I am very gay.' Then he took his valise, and his books under his arm, and kissed her quickly and opened the door, and there was his friend coming up the stairs. She closed the door then, leaning against it."

# The Memoirs of Casanova

## Italo Calvino

Throughout my stay at ———— I had two steady lovers: Cate and Ilda. Cate came to see me every morning, Ilda in the afternoon; in the evening I went out socializing and people were amazed to see me always on my own. Cate was well-built, Ilda was slim; going from one to the other renewed desire, which tends as much to variation as to repetition.

Once Cate had left I hid every trace of her; likewise with Ilda; and I think I always managed to stop either of them finding out about the other, both at the time and perhaps afterwards too.

Of course I would sometimes slip up and say things to one of them that could only mean something if said to the other: 'I found these fuchsias at the florist today, your favourite flower,' or 'Don't forget to take your necklace again,' thus provoking amazement, anger, suspicion. But these banal improprieties only occurred, if I well remember, at the beginning of the double affair. Very soon I learnt to separate the two relationships completely; each relationship took its course, had its continuity of conversations and habits, and never interfered with the other.

At the beginning I thought (I was, as you will have appreciated, very young, and looking for experience) that amatory arts would be transferable from one woman to the other: both knew a great deal more than me and I thought that the secrets I learnt from Ilda I would then be able to teach to Cate, and vice versa.

I was wrong: all I did was to muddle things that are only valuable when spontaneous and direct. Each woman was a world unto herself, or rather each was a sky where I must trace the positions of stars, planets, orbits, eclipses, inclinations and conjunctions, solstice and equinox. Each firmament had its own movement, in line with its own mechanism and rhythm. I couldn't expect to apply notions of astronomy I'd learnt watching Cate's sky, to Ilda's.

But I must confess that freedom of choice between two lines of behaviour was no longer an option: with Cate I had been trained to act one way and with Ilda another; I was conditioned in every way by the partner I was with, to the extent that even my instinctive preferences and tics would change. Two personalities alternated inside me; and I wouldn't have been able to say which me was really me.

What I've said holds good as much for the spirit as the body: the words spoken to the one couldn't be repeated to the other, and I very soon realized I would have to vary my way of thinking too.

When I feel the urge to recount and evoke one of the many twists and turns of my adventurous life, I usually resort to the well-tried versions I've developed for social occasions, with whole sentences and more repeated word for word, the effects calculated right down to the digressions and pauses. But certain escapades that never failed to win the appreciation of groups of people who didn't know me, or who weren't involved, had to be considerably adapted if I was to tell them to Cate or Ilda alone. Certain expressions that were common currency with Cate, sounded wrong when I was with Ilda; the quips Ilda picked up at once and returned with interest, I would have had to explain to Cate with every 'i' dotted and 't' crossed, though she appreciated other jokes that left Ilda cold; sometimes it was the conclusion to be drawn from a story that changed from Ilda to Cate, so that I took to giving my stories different endings. In this way I was gradually constructing two different versions of my life.

Every day I would tell Cate and Ilda what I had seen and heard the evening before wandering round the haunts and hangouts in town: gossip, shows, celebrities, fashionable clothes, eccentricities. In my early days of undifferentiated insensibility, I would repeat word for word to Ilda in the afternoon whatever I'd said in the morning to Cate: I thought this would save me the imaginative effort one is constantly having to make to keep people interested. I soon realized that the same story either interested one and not the other, or, if it interested both, then the details they asked for were different and likewise different were the comments and judgements they expressed.

What I had to do then was to produce two quite different stories from the same material: and this wouldn't have been particularly problematic; except that each evening I also had to live through things in two different ways in line with the stories I'd be telling the following morning; I'd look at everything and everybody from Cate's point of view and from Ilda's point of view, and I'd judge them in line with their two different criteria; in conversation I'd come up with two retorts to the same quip from someone else, one that Ilda would like, the other that Cate would like; every retort generated counter-retorts that I had to reply to once again in two ways. I wasn't aware of this split personality operating when I was in the company of one or the other of them, but mostly when they weren't there.

My mind had become the two women's battlefield. Cate and Ilda, who didn't know of each other outside my head, were constantly clashing and fighting for territory inside me, hitting out at each other, tearing each other to shreds. The sole purpose of my existence was to be host to the bitter struggle between two rivals neither of whom knew anything about it.

That was the real reason that persuaded me to leave ——— in a hurry, never to return.

## 2

I was attracted to Irma because she reminded me of Dirce. I sat next to her: she just had to turn her body a little towards me and put a hand over her face (I would whisper to her; she would laugh) and the illusion of being close to Dirce was striking. The illusion awoke memories, the memories desires. To transmit them to Irma somehow, I gripped her hand. Her touch and the way she started revealed her to me for what she was, different. This sensation was stronger than the other, but without cancelling it out, and, in itself, agreeable. I realized that I would be able to derive a double pleasure from Irma: that of pursuing through her the lost Dirce, and that of allowing myself to be surprised by an unfamiliar presence.

Every desire traces its curve within us, a line that climbs, wavers, sometimes dissolves. The line the absent woman evoked in me might, a second before it began to decline, intersect with the line of my curiosity in the present woman, and transmit its upward thrust to this still all undiscovered trajectory. The plan was worth a try: I redoubled my attentiveness in Irma's regard, until I persuaded her to come to my room at night.

She came in. She let her cloak slip off. She was wearing a

light white muslin blouse that the wind (it being spring the window was open) ruffled. That was when I realized that a different and unexpected mechanism was taking charge of my sensations and thoughts. It was Irma who was taking up the whole field of my attention, Irma as a unique and unrepeatable person, skin and voice and eyes, while the resemblances to Dirce that occasionally surfaced in my mind were no more than a disturbance, so much so that I was eager to be rid of them.

Hence my meeting with Irma became a battle with the shade of Dirce who kept on sneaking in between us, and every time I felt I was about to capture the indefinable essence of Irma, every time I felt I had established an intimacy between us that excluded every other presence or thought, back came Dirce, or the past experience that Dirce embodied for me, to stamp her impression on what I was experiencing that very moment and prevent me from feeling it as new. At this point Dirce, her memory, the mark she had made on me, brought me nothing but annoyance, constraint, boredom.

Dawn was coming in through the shutter slats in blades of pearl-grey light, when I realized beyond any doubt that my night with Irma was not the one now about to end, but another night like this one, a night still to come when I would seek the memory of Irma in another woman, and suffer first when I found her again and when I lost her again, and then when I couldn't free myself from her.

3

I rediscovered Tullia twenty years on. Chance, which in the past had brought us together only to separate us just when we realized we liked each other, now finally allowed us to pick up the thread of our relationship at the point where it had broken off. 'You haven't changed at all,' we both told each other. Were we lying? Not entirely: 'I haven't changed,' was what both she and I wished to have the other understand.

This time the relationship developed as both expected. At first it was Tullia's mature beauty which engaged all my attention, and only later did I tell myself not to forget the young Tullia, seeking to recover the continuity between the two. Hence, playing a game that came to us spontaneously when we talked, we would pretend that our separation had lasted twenty-four hours and not twenty years, and that our memories were of things that had happened only the day before. It was lovely, but it wasn't true. If I thought of myself as I was then with her as she was then, I was confronted with two strangers; they aroused warmth, affection, plenty of it, tenderness too, but what I was able to imagine in their regard had nothing to do with what Tullia and I were now.

Of course we still regretted how all too brief our first encounter had been. Was it the natural regret for lost youth? But my present satisfaction I felt gave me no cause for regret; and Tullia too, now I was getting to know her, was a woman too taken up with the present to abandon herself to nostalgia. Regret for what we hadn't been able to have then? Maybe a little, but not entirely: because (again with this exclusive enthusiasm for what the present was giving us) I felt (perhaps wrongly) that if our desire had been satisfied at once it might have removed something from our happiness today. If anything the regret had to do with what those two poor youngsters, those 'others', had lost, and was added to the sum of all the losses the world suffers in every instant never to retrieve. From the height of our sudden richness, we deigned to cast a compassionate eye on those excluded: hardly a disinterested feeling, since it allowed us to savour our privilege the better.

Two opposing conclusions can be drawn from my relationship with Tullia. One might say that having found each other again cancelled out the separation of twenty years before, erased the loss we suffered; and one might say on the contrary that it rendered that loss decisive, desperate. Those two (Tullia and I as we were then) had lost each other for ever, never to meet again, and in vain would they have called on the Tullia and I of today for help, since we (the selfishness of happy lovers is boundless) had entirely forgotten them.

4

Of other women I remember a gesture, a repeated expression, an inflexion, that were intimately bound up with the essence of the person and distinguished them like a signature. Not so with Sofia. Or rather, I remember a great deal about Sofia, too much perhaps: eyelids, calves, a belt, a perfume, many preferences and obsessions, the songs she knew, an obscure confession, some dreams; all things my memory still keeps in its store and links with her but which are doomed to be lost because I can't find the thread that binds them together and I don't know which of them contains the real Sofia. Between each detail lies a gap; and taken one by one, they might just as well be attributed to someone else as to her. As for our lovemaking (we met in secret for months), I remember that it was different every time, and although this should be a positive quality for someone like myself who fears the blunting effect of habit, it now turns out to be a fault, since I can't remember what prompted me to go to her rather than anyone else each time I went. In short, I don't remember anything at all.

Perhaps all I wanted to understand about her at the beginning was whether I liked her or not: that was why the first time I saw her I bombarded her with questions, some of them indiscreet. Instead of fending these off, which she could well have done, in reply to every question she overwhelmed me with all kinds of clarifications, revelations and allusions, at once fragmentary and digressive, while I, in my struggle to keep up with her and hold on to what she was telling me, got more and more lost. Result: it was as if she hadn't answered me at all.

To establish communication in a different language I risked a caress. In response Sofia's movements were entirely aimed at containing and putting off my assault, if not exactly rejecting it, with the result that the moment one part of her body slipped away from my hand, my fingers would slither on to another, her evasion thus leading me to carry out an exploration of her skin at once fragmentary yet extensive. In short, the information gathered through touch was no less abundant than that recorded by hearing, albeit equally incoherent.

Nothing remained but to complete our acquaintance on every level and as soon as possible. But was it one unique woman this person who undressed before me, removing both the visible and invisible clothes the ways of the world impose on us, or was it many women in one? And which of these was it that attracted me, which that put me off? There was never an occasion when I didn't discover something I wasn't expecting in Sofia, and less and less would I have been able to answer that first question I had asked myself: did I or didn't I like her?

Today, going over it in my memory, another doubt occurs: is it that when a woman hides nothing of herself I am incapable of understanding her; or is it that Sofia in revealing herself so abundantly was deploying a sophisticated strategy for not letting me capture her? And I tell myself of all of them, she was the one who got away, as if I had never had her. But did I really have her? And then I ask myself: and who did I really have? And then again: have who? what? what does it mean?

## 5

I met Fulvia at the right moment: as chance would have it I was the first man in her young life. Unfortunately this lucky encounter was destined to be brief; circumstances obliged me to leave town; my ship was already in harbour; the next morning it was due to set sail.

We were both aware that we would not see each other again, and equally aware that this was part of the established and ineluctable order of things; hence the sadness we felt, though to differing degrees, was governed, once again to differing degrees, by reason. Fulvia already sensed the emptiness she would feel when our new and barely begun familiarity was broken off, but also the freedom this would open up for her and the many opportunities it would provide; I on the other hand had a habit of placing the events of my life in a pattern where the present receives light and shade from the future, a future whose trajectory in this case I could already imagine right up to its decline: what I foresaw for Fulvia was the full flowering of an amorous vocation which I had helped to awaken.

Hence in those last dallyings before our farewell I couldn't help seeing myself as merely the first of the long series of lovers. Fulvia was doubtless going to have, and to reassess what had happened between us in the light of her future experiences. I realized that every last detail of a passion that Fulvia had surrendered herself to with total abandon would be remembered and judged by the woman she would become in just a few years' time. As things stood now, Fulvia accepted everything about me without judging: but the day was not far off when she would be able to compare me with other men; every memory of me would be subjected to parallels, distinctions, judgements. I had before me an as yet inexperienced girl for whom I represented all that could be known, but all the same I felt I was being watched by the Fulvia of tomorrow, demanding and disenchanted.

My first reaction was one of fear of comparison. Fulvia's future men, I thought, would be capable of making her fall totally in love with them, as she had not been with me. Sooner or later Fulvia would deem me unworthy of the fortune that had befallen me; it would be disappointment and sarcasm that kept alive her memory of me: I envied my nameless successors, I sensed that they were already lying in wait, ready to snatch Fulvia away, I hated them, and already I hated her too because Fate had already destined her for them ...

To escape this pain, I reversed the train of my thoughts, passing from self-detraction to self-praise. It wasn't hard: by temperament I am rather inclined to forming a high opinion of myself than a low. Fulvia had had an invaluable stroke of luck meeting me first; but taking me as a model would expose her to cruel disappointments. Other men she would meet would seem crude, feeble, dull and dumb, after myself. In her innocence she no doubt imagined my good qualities to be fairly common attributes amongst my sex; I must warn her that seeking from others what she had found in me could only lead to disillusionment. I shivered in horror at the thought that after such a happy beginning Fulvia might fall into unworthy hands, who would harm her, maim her, debase her. I hated all of them; and I ended up hating her too because destiny was to snatch her from me condemning her to a degraded future.

One way or another, the passion that had me in its grip was, I suspect, the one I have always heard described as 'jealousy', a mental disturbance from which I had imagined circumstances had rendered me immune. Having established that I was jealous, all I could do was behave like a jealous man. I lost my temper with Fulvia, telling her I couldn't stand her being so calm just before we were about to part; I accused her of hardly being able to wait to betray me; I was unkind to her, cruel. But she (no doubt out of inexperience) seemed to find this change in my mood natural and wasn't unduly upset. Very sensibly she advised me not to waste the little time we had left together on pointless recriminations.

Then I knelt at her feet, I begged her to pardon me, not to inveigh too bitterly against me when she had found a companion worthy of her; I hoped for no greater indulgence than to be forgotten. She treated me as though I were mad; she wouldn't let me speak of what had happened between us in anything but the most flattering terms; otherwise, she said, it spoiled the effect.

This served to reassure me as to my image, but then I found myself commiserating with Fulvia over her future destiny: other men were worthless; I should warn her that the fullness she'd known with me wouldn't happen again with anyone else. She answered that she too felt sorry for me, because our happiness came from our being together, once apart we would both lose it; but to preserve it for some time longer we should both immerse ourselves in it totally without imagining we could define it from without.

The conclusion I came to from without, waving my handkerchief to her from the ship as the anchor was raised, was this: the experience that had entirely occupied Fulvia all the time she was with me was not the discovery of myself and not even the discovery of love or of men, but of herself; even in my absence this discovery, once begun, would never cease; I had only been an instrument.

# Art History

Michelle Cliff

I pick up the *New York Times* sometime in 1992 and find your name. My heart catches. We are twenty years from a summer filled with each other, and now I hear you laugh, and I sound foolishly romantic, now death is around us.

The first winnowing, a doctor said, cold. And if she is right, who will be left standing? This feels like a rout.

Riding uptown in a cab one spring evening in 1990—it's important to get the years right; so much is happening, so fast—passing a bar called Billy's Topless; Angela musing, "I wonder if his mother knows?"

Arturo laughing.

Me between the two of them. She and I get out in the thirties, Arturo heads farther uptown. He's convinced the hotel's haunted by the ghost of Veronica Lake.

Two years later both he and Angela are dead.

"I'll call you when I'm in London."

His huge eyes. "We need a party."

But talk of that is for another time.

That summer you were subletting the apartment of an art historian in a brownstone just off Park, verging Spanish Harlem. Almost the top of the City, where the streets begin to broaden, becoming lighter, darker.

The art historian sent you a postcard from the Bomarzo, showing a picnic table between the legs of a gigantic stucco, stone, or terra cotta female. Her message was all business, then, underlined, "My favorite place to dine when in Italy." You showed it to me without a word.

The color in my cheeks rose higher and higher.

You were smiling. "Just once?" you asked.

I turned away, to the windows at the front of the apartment, overlooking the street, a playground, and some tenement walls plastered with Colt 45 and Newport ads in Spanish, and one wall that stood apart. On it shreds of a couple dressed in evening clothes framed a portrait of Bessie Smith. Someone had cast the Empress across brick, across ancient lettering advertising Madam's Rosewater, worn into "adam's Rose," elixir disappearing into her ermine wrap.

The light of the summer evening set the street to glowing, bathing the girls and boys in the playground, the men leaning against the anchor fence, the brown bags housing Ripple or Night Train or Thunderbird. Bessie Smith watching over them all. For a minute everything was golden, and then the evening shadows crept in.

"There's nothing like summer in New York," I said. I turned around and kissed you goodbye.

"Why don't you stay?"

I was living downtown, in the Village, housesitting the townhouse of a former boss, whose copper-topped cocktail table I kept polished, whose mail I collected, and whose very gray portrait hung over the mantelpiece. She was perched on the edge of a chair, leaning forward, out of the plane of the picture, almost to launch herself into the room.

Her eyes were the same color as the suit she was posed in, close to charcoal, oddly missing the pinpoints of white, the light captive in the eye.

The painting was signed by her husband.

"Bill so much wanted a son," she told me as she showed me around the house, "and look what he got." We had ended up on the top floor of the slender building, in her son's room; painted black, with a purple ceiling, without furniture. "Absence," she said.

About a year before she had taken me to lunch at the Algonquin for my birthday. Because, she explained, they had the driest martinis in a five-block radius. I'd revealed to her that I'd never had a martini, and she said, "My God, you can't call yourself an American and not have had a martini."

She meant well and went ahead and ordered for me.

After she had drunk about three of them, she told me about her boy, actually a man, who set fire to the brooms at the Montessori where he worked as an aide. She talked about his need to fall from higher and higher places. She thought he was trying to fly, she said. "To leave himself behind and rise from the ashes.

"But it was no good."

After years of high places, and the places beneath, he fell from a window in Macy's, where he worked as a stockboy.

"One of those rainy New York nights," she said, "in November."

All of a sudden I thought of the Thanksgiving Day Parade and in my mind's eye caught a boy entangled in the guy wires of a balloon. Popeye's tattooed forearm floated by. I wanted to smile. It must have been the gin.

"I had to identify him. The morgue people didn't know what to do with me. They just stared, as if to ask, what kind of a woman has a son like that?"

I tried to engage her eyes but she was staring into her glass, into the bluish tinge of good gin.

"I didn't actually see what the fall had done. They had covered his face. I identified him from the nametag on his smock. But they told me."

I did not know what to say to her, except, "I'm sorry." It was one of those moments when I felt ignorant of some secret female gesture, something traditional I had never learned.

"Thank you," she said, "but I've only myself to blame." For what? I wondered. Not breast-feeding him? Being a "career-woman"? Not wanting a child in the first place?

"Why should you blame yourself?" I asked, using the

same tone I had learned to use with my father when he drank too much and became maudlin. I hated the sound of it, matching the unrealness of the drunken voice note for note.

"I should never have listened to them."

"Who?"

"The doctors. My husband. You have no idea how difficult artists can be. The last thing he wanted . . "

"Oh," I said, unable to ask what.

"It was the fifties." She paused. Specters crowded in. "I like Ikea" Betty Furness opening a sparkling white Westinghouse. *I've Got a Secret.*

"I didn't have a hell of a lot of options. Punishment and reward. That was the prescription. Please don't tell anyone about this."

"Of course not."

I wasn't sure what I'd heard.

I went back to my office, closed the door, and fell asleep.

We were standing in his room, at the top of the slender house, the door open to the fire escape, the perfect perch for a boy who wanted to fly.

In the purple ceiling and black walls were thumbtack marks, and I wondered what he had pinned there and what they would tell me if I knew.

She broke the silence in the room.

"There's one other thing about housesitting this summer. I probably should have mentioned this to you before."

"What is it?"

"If my son calls here you are under no circumstances to tell him where we are." She was cold sober, and her voice was un-wavering although gathering speed. "And, if he asks to come here, you are to tell him no, in no uncertain terms. If he per-sists, or tries to get in, first call the precinct—they know all about the situation—then call us."

It had started to rain, a summer shower, sounding on the roof right over us, pelting the railing of the fire escape. The hot scent of summer mixing with rain came into the room, and she went on about the dead-alive boy.

I was, as they say in old novels, nonplussed.

"Damn, Bill and I better get going. He hates to drive in bad weather. The number in Wellfleet is by the phone in the kitchen. This is the first time in years Bill and I have had a place without room for Billy. There's no place for him with us anymore, there just isn't. Here, there, anywhere. You do understand, don't you?"

Hardly. But I nodded anyway, and when I found my voice I assured her, "Yes." I knew enough not to ask.

"Oh, and I'll leave a photo of him by the phone. It's a bit out of date, but it's the only one left. For God's sake don't fall for his poor soul routine."

"I won't," I said, and felt horrible.

As soon as they drove off I went into the kitchen. On a bul-letin board next to the wall phone, between a postcard of a lighthouse and the takeout menu from the Good Woman of

Szechuan, was the photograph of a boy. Dark, as if it had been taken at night with a flash. Crewcut, striped polo shirt, two-wheeler, vintage 1955 or so.

The landscape around the boy was nondescript. It could have been anywhere a boy like him might have been.

Central Park, maybe. Just some bushes and trees. In the darkness it was hard to tell much more. No suggestion of water, no shadow of a city skyline.

When I showed it to you, you thought he might be standing on the grounds of the place in *I Never Promised You a Rose Garden* or some other upper-class madhouse. Like Cascades in *Now Voyager*. Ice cream, tennis, Claude Rains.

"Where rich people send their kids," you said. "Then why did she say … ?"

"She'd had a lot to drink. Maybe she has a drunken version and a sober version. Maybe she wishes he would."

"Jump?"

"Umhmm."

"Or maybe he's been standing by these bushes for twenty years."

I had no idea what I would do should he try to get in touch. I put the photograph away, in a drawer with playing cards and flashlight batteries.

I took the portrait from over the mantelpiece and hid it in a closet.

It was no use. Their shadows overwhelmed the place. I began spending more and more time uptown, returning to West

11th only to erase the tarnish from the coppertopped cocktail table and collect the mail.

One day there was a bill from someplace in the Berkshires, stamped *dated material, please respond* and the mystery seemed to be solved.

No matter.


I slept with you in the art historian's bed, under a print of Michelangelo's *Night*. We slept like children at first.

But soon I woke to find my hand in the small of your back, finger there, becoming aware of your skin and mine. The evenness of your breath. The only sound in a room in a city with the windows open.

"What are you afraid of?" you asked me in the dawn.

"I want your mouth on me."

"Oh, that." You laughed in half-sleep.

Drawing me closer.


The art historian sent a postcard from a bar called Elle Est Lui. "I hope you've met my neighbors by now." Then: "*Toujours gai!*" signed Mehitabel.

Downstairs, in the garden apartment, were two painters, Judith and Alberto. She from Grand Island, Nebraska. He from a hilltown near Siena.

The art historian had not mentioned that Judith was dying.

As Alberto cooked, Judith talked almost nonstop, as if silence was a passage into the dark.

At first she entertained us with art world gossip. "Louise? Forget her. She just calls the foundry now. Doesn't even bother to stop by."

One of us mentioned the name of another woman artist, exploding into posters, calendars, notecards, threatening even Warhol with her promiscuity.

Judith smiled. "What's next?" she asked. "Sheets and pillow-cases? A shower curtain with one of her wretched cow skulls?

"And she's never been sick a day in her life. Imagine. Just imagine."

As Judith spoke, the colored lights around the fountain in the back garden flickered. The water sprayed through the lights from the wide-open mouth of a dolphin, creating tiny, constantly changing patterns. The relentless exchange of form and color, light and water, helped take her mind off the pain, which the painkillers did less and less to mask.

We began to stop by there almost every evening.

"Here," she said suddenly, "this really belongs to you. I want you to have it."

She handed me a copy of *Wide Sargasso Sea*.

I looked at the jacket. A sad-looking young woman stood in the middle of an explosion of tropical lushness. She held a red hibiscus blossom. "Why?" I asked Judith. I didn't know the book at all.

"Because it's about your part of the world," she said. "How amazing to come from a place like that."

I only nodded, not having the heart to tell her what I actually thought of paradise. On the back of the book jacket was a familiar sight, the great house about to be swallowed by the green.

"Alberto and I were there once."

"Really? When?"

"A long time ago. Kingston was one of our ports of call on a voyage way back when. We took a freighter. We were only allowed to spend one afternoon ashore. When we got back the decks were piled high with bananas. And we were off, doing the bidding of United Fruit. I remember the mountains as this green approaching blue and the sea, my God ... in the harbor dolphins skated by us. I was sitting on a pile of bananas, sketching like crazy. What must it have been like being a girl there?"

I always become wary when someone not of my ilk speaks of Jamaica, especially if I like the person. I wait for smiling or sullen natives, simple or crafty marketwomen, paradise lost on its inhabitants.

"It *is* a beautiful place," I said.

"I'm only sorry we weren't there long enough to get a real sense of it. We did see the boys diving for coins alongside the cruise ships. That was distressing."

I remembered those boys. There, as if they should be. Like the coconut palms, Her Majesty's sailors on leave, the maze at Hope Gardens, the viciousness of peacocks. Nothing was said in that part of the world when I was a girl. A truckful of marketwomen falling into a ravine. Screams into a Saturday night, then silence. I remember the headlights shining from below. People spoke of how the roadway was haunted, nothing else.

I was about to let her into a sliver of my girlhood, then I realized she had dozed off.

Judith didn't want any of her old friends or rivals "to see me like this," or so she said. Maybe she was afraid to ask them. I wondered if the remark about Louise not bothering to stop by referred to the foundry after all.

She said she was content with our company. "My new friends, my girls. You know, I don't believe anyone dies of cancer. Not as long as you have company."

"You're probably right," you said.

"Yes," Judith said. "You have to be alone to die."

My mother had been. Maybe Judith was right.

I allowed myself the chance to look at you, your amber eyes rapt with her blue ones. I watched you take her hand, your fingers cradling hers, resting on the thing that covered her. She sighed. She gripped you tightly.

We sat there until the terror passed. For now.

"We should probably be going," I whispered, and you nodded, and that afternoon under the print of *Night* I made love to you, lifting and parting, lifting and parting, drinking you to my heart's content.

The next day we met for lunch in midtown and afterwards strolled through the Morgan Library. A guard showed us the murals in the ceiling over the old man's desk. Angelic or pagan forms gaped down, colors fading into wormed wood but for bright gilt around the borders. "From Lucca, Italy," the guard said, as if it were his ceiling, "I can tell you anything you want to know."

Judith sat across from her water and lights as Alberto cooked us chanterelles he'd gathered behind the reservoir in Central Park.

"Alberto goes mushroom gathering every day the day after it rains," she said.

The City had been washed clean the day before, that kind of hot rain that falls in August.

"Isn't this marvelous?" she asked us, holding up a tumbler. "They gave it to Alberto at a gas station."

GIANTS was stenciled on the side of the glass in dark blue along with a football helmet.

"Alberto goes mushroom gathering and he also digs potatoes and onions. Guess where."

We both looked blank.

"Give up?"

"On one of those truck farms on Long Island," I guessed.

"Nope." She couldn't wait to tell us. "On the grounds of the Cloisters," she paused. "Honest."

"I kid you not," Alberto attested.

"Someone's kitchen garden from a long time ago. When the place was rural, before they put that pile of stones there. Imagine. Who were they? Whatever remains concealed in the middle of some bushes. The sweetest onions you've ever tasted. And the potatoes! My God. A kind from before all the crap they put into the ground. Some gnarled, misshapen, dented where they grew against rock. Nothing perfect."

"How did you find them?" I asked Alberto.

"I smelled the onions one afternoon. Very strong. I followed my nose to them. In Italian, *cipollini*."

"And garlic," Judith said, "and thyme and sage. Lavender. Don't you love the City? I find it very moving. Chamomile coming up through cobblestones."

"All through the City you find things like this," Alberto said.

"Anyplace people have lived a long time," Judith said. "There are vineyards in the depths of Staten Island."

It was a beautiful vision. The City as garden. The traces of others.

"Please come to dinner on Sunday," Judith invited us.

"Prego," Alberto said.

"Alberto has promised to trap a rabbit in Westchester—not as crazy as it sounds—and roast it on a spit in the fireplace for us. We'll put on the air conditioning full blast and pretend we're in the middle of a Russian winter instead of a waning New York summer. We must each choose someone to be. Someone who doesn't have cancer, that is."

"How about TB?" you asked, and Judith smiled.

"Yes, poor wretches, they all coughed, didn't they? All through those interminable novels—that or epilepsy, the Idiot and all that. No, we must be healthy Russians. No bloody handkerchiefs. Picture Catherine the Great, robust as hell I have no doubt."

"Can we bring anything?" I asked.

"Just yourselves. You may choose to be lovers." She smiled up at us from her place on the couch.

"It's the drugs talking; you must excuse her," Alberto said.

"It is not, my darling; not at all."

You bent over her and kissed her, we said good night and turned to go upstairs.

"Just steer clear of Anna and Vronsky. Talk about the wrong side of the tracks." She laughed.

I stood at the bedroom window for a long time, looking out over Judith's fountain, the lights playing through the water, the water flowing from the dolphin. As long as there was light and motion I felt safe for her.

And then Alberto turned out the lights, shut off the flow of water, and I knew Judith had fallen asleep. That's how it would be. I hoped as much.

"Were you surprised?" You had come up behind me, your arm was around my middle.

"A little. Is it that obvious?"

"I do think she cares about us, you know."

"I just don't like having my mind read, that's all."

"Don't read disapproval into what she said, unless it's your own."

Boom! There it was, and I couldn't say anything.

You were looking into the darkness as the night breezes swung into the art historian's bedroom, lifting the corners of

*Night.* The traffic noises, the breaking of glass across the way seemed to back off, and instead we heard Bessie Smith, her fine sounds, her blues.

The night with its half-asleep sounds, then the suddenness of the human voice raised in caress.

Sunday, as promised, a rabbit turned slowly on the spit, its fur wrapping to one side, folded in anticipation of another use.

Alberto wasted nothing.

He was at the sink blending a wild berry mixture into some yogurt.

Judith was all dressed up. Not as a Russian; that scheme had been forgotten, or discarded. She was dressed as if for a gallery opening, all in black with a bright scarf wrapped around her burned head.

Around her, facing her on the tile of the kitchen floor, was her life's work.

One canvas was yellow. A bright chrome yellow. In the middle the painting seemed to tear and an underlayer of paint was revealed. Apparition of black beneath yellow. Dark behind light.

II

Judith died that September. In the middle of an Indian summer heatwave when there was a power failure and the lights around the City went out.

Stars were visible. The moon hung over the men in the playground.

The art historian returned from her travels with a woman she'd found at the Sound and Light show at the Colosseum in Rome.

My former boss sent a postcard of Highland Light and asked if I'd guard the townhouse one more month. "Bill and I have found each other again," she wrote, "who knows where this might lead?" P.S.: "We're thinking of adopting."

I ignored her request and called the precinct to tell them I had been called away and left the keys to the house with Captain January or whatever his name was.

# Mr. Tennyson

## William Trevor

He had, romantically, a bad reputation. He had a wife and several children. His carry-on with Sarah Spence was a legend among a generation of girls, and the story was that none of it had stopped with Sarah Spence. His old red Ford Escort had been reported drawn up in quiet lay-bys; often he spent weekends away from home; Annie Green had come across him going somewhere on a train once, alone and morose in the buffet car. Nobody's parents were aware of the facts about him, nor were the other staff, nor even the boys at the school. His carry-on with Sarah Spence, and coming across him or his car, made a little tapestry of secrets that suddenly was yours when you became fifteen and a senior, a member of 2A. For the rest of your time at Foxton Comprehensive—for the rest of your life, preferably—you didn't breathe a word to people whose business it wasn't.

It was understandable when you looked at him that parents and staff didn't guess. It was also understandable that his activities were protected by the senior girls. He was forty years old. He had dark hair with a little grey in it, and a face that was boyish—like a French boy's, someone had once said, and the description had stuck, often to be repeated. There was a kind of ragamuffin innocence about his eyes. The cast of his lips suggested a melancholy nature and his smile, when it came, had sadness in it too. His name was Mr Tennyson. His subject was English.

Jenny, arriving one September in 2A, learnt all about him. She remembered Sarah Spence, a girl at the top of the school when she had been at the bottom, tall and beautiful. He carried on because he was unhappily married, she was informed. Consider where he lived even: trapped in tiny gate-lodge on the Ilminster road because he couldn't afford anything better, trapped with a wife and children when he deserved freedom. Would he one day publish poetry as profound as his famous namesake's, though of course more up-to-date? Or was his talent lost for ever? One way or the other he was made for love.

It seemed to Jenny that the girls of 2A eyed one another, wondering which among them would become a successor to Sarah Spence. They eyed the older girls, of Class 1, 1A and 1B, wondering which of them was already her successor, discreetly taking her place in the red Ford Escort on dusky afternoons. He would never be coarse, you couldn't imagine coarseness in him. He'd never try anything unpleasant, he'd never in a million years fumble at you. He'd just be there, being himself, smelling faintly of fresh tobacco, the fingers of a hand perhaps brushing your arm by accident.

'Within the play,' he suggested in his soft voice, almost a whisper, 'order is represented by the royal house of Scotland. We must try and remember Shakespeare's point of view, how Shakespeare saw these things.'

They were studying *Macbeth* and *Huckleberry Finn* with him, but when he talked about Shakespeare it seemed more natural and suited to him than when he talked about Mark Twain.

'On Duncan's death,' he said, 'should the natural order continue, his son Malcolm would become king. Already Duncan has indicated—by making Malcolm Prince of Cumberland—that he considers him capable of ruling.'

Jenny had pale fair hair, the colour of ripened wheat. It fell from a divide at the centre of her head, two straight lines on either side of a thin face. Her eyes were large and of a faded blue. She was lanky, with legs she considered to be too long but which her mother said she'd be thankful for one day.

'Disruption is everywhere, remember,' he said. 'Disruption in nature as well as in the royal house. Shakespeare insinuates a comparison between what is happening in human terms and in terms of nature. On the night of Duncan's death there is a sudden storm in which chimneys are blown off and houses shaken. Mysterious screams are heard. Horses go wild. A falcon is killed by a mousing owl.'

Listening to him, it seemed to Jenny that she could listen for ever, no matter what he said. At night, lying in bed with her eyes closed, she delighted in leisurely fantasies, of having breakfast with him and ironing his clothes, of walking beside him on a seashore or sitting beside him in his old Ford Escort. There was a particular story she repeated to herself: that she was on the promenade at Lyme Regis and that he came up to her and asked her if she'd like to go for a walk. They walked up to the cliffs and then along the cliff-path, and everything was different from Foxton Comprehensive because they were alone together. His wife and he had been divorced, he told her, having agreed between themselves that they were incompatible. He was leaving Foxton Comprehensive because a play he'd written was going to be done on the radio and another one on the London stage. 'Oh, darling,' she said, daring to say it. 'Oh, Jenny,' he said.

Terms and holidays went by. Once, just before the Easter of that year, she met him with his wife, shopping in the International Stores in Ilminster. They had two of their four children with them, little boys with freckles. His wife had freckles also. She was a woman like a sack of something, Jenny considered, with thick, unhealthy-looking legs. He was pushing a trolley full of breakfast cereals and wrapped bread, and tins. Although he didn't speak to her or even appear to see her, it was a stroke of luck to come across him in the town because he didn't often come into the village. Foxton had only half a dozen shops and the Bow and Arrow public house even though it was enormous, a sprawling dormitory village that had had the new Comprehensive added to all the other new building in 1969. Because of the position of the Tennysons' gate-lodge it was clearly more convenient for them to shop in Ilminster.

'Hullo, Mr Tennyson,' she said in the International Stores, and he turned and looked at her. He nodded and smiled.

Jenny moved into 1A at the end of that school year. She wondered if he'd noticed how her breasts had become bigger during the time she'd been in 2A, and how her complexion had definitely improved. Her breasts were quite presentable now, which was a relief because she'd had a fear that they weren't going to develop at all. She wondered if he'd noticed her Green Magic eye-shadow. Everyone said it suited her, except her father, who always blew up over things like that. Once she heard one of the new kids saying she was the prettiest girl in the school. Adam Swann and Chinny Martin from 1B kept hanging about, trying to chat her up. Chinny Martin even wrote her notes.

'You're mooning,' her father said. 'You don't take a pick of notice these days.'

'Exams,' her mother hastily interjected and afterwards, when Jenny was out of the room, quite sharply reminded her husband that adolescence was a difficult time for girls. It was best not to remark on things.

'I didn't mean a criticism, Ellie,' Jenny's father protested, aggrieved.

'They take it as a criticism. Every word. They're edgy, see.'

He sighed. He was a painter and decorator, with his own business. Jenny was their only child. There'd been four miscarriages, all of which might have been boys, which naturally were what he'd wanted, with the business. He'd have to sell it one day, but it didn't matter all that much when you thought about it. Having miscarriages was worse than selling a business, more depressing really. A woman's lot was harder than a man's, he'd decided long ago.

'Broody,' his wife diagnosed. 'Just normal broody. She'll see her way through it.'

Every evening her parents sat in their clean, neat sitting-room watching television. Her mother made tea at nine o'-clock because it was nice to have a cup with the news. She always called upstairs to Jenny, but Jenny never wanted to have tea or see the news. She did her homework in her bedroom, a small room that was clean and neat also, with a pebbly cream wallpaper expertly hung by her father. At half past ten she usually went down to the kitchen and made herself some Ovaltine. She drank it at the table with the cat, Tinkle, on her lap. Her mother usually came in with the tea things to wash up, and then might chat, the conversation consisting mainly of gossip from Foxton Comprehensive, although never of course containing a reference to Mr Tennyson. Sometimes Jenny didn't feel like chatting and wouldn't, feigning sleepiness. If she sat there long enough her father would come in to fetch himself a cup of water because he always liked to have one near him in the night. He couldn't help glancing at her eye-shadow when he said good-night and she could see him making an effort not to mention it, having doubtless been told not to by her mother. They did their best. She liked them very much. She loved them, she supposed.

But not in the way she loved Mr Tennyson. 'Robert Tennyson,' she murmured to herself in bed. 'Oh, Robert dear.' Softly his lips were there, and the smell of fresh tobacco made her swoon, forcing her to close her eyes. 'Oh, yes,' she said. 'Oh, yes, yes.' He lifted the dress over her head. His hands were taut, charged with their shared passion. 'My love,' he said in his soft voice, almost a whisper. Every night before she went to sleep his was the face that entirely filled her mind. Had it once not been there she would have thought herself faithless. And every morning, in a ceremonial way, she conjured it up again, first thing, pride of place.

Coming out of Harper's the newsagent's one Saturday afternoon, she found waiting for her, not Mr Tennyson, but Chinny Martin, with his motor-cycle on its pedestal in the street. He asked her if she'd like to go for a spin into the country and offered to supply her with a crash helmet. He was wearing a crash helmet himself, a bulbous red object with a peak and a windshield that fitted over his eyes. He was also wearing heavy plastic gloves, red also, and a red windcheater. He was smiling at her, the spots on his pronounced chin more noticeable after exposure to the weather on his motor-cycle. His eyes were serious, closely fixed on hers.

She shook her head at him. There was hardly anything she'd have disliked more than a ride into the country with Chinny Martin, her arms half round his waist, a borrowed crash helmet making her feel silly. He'd stop the motor-cycle in a suitable place and he'd suggest something like a walk to the river or to some old ruin or into a wood. He'd suggest sitting down and then he'd begin to fumble at her, and his chin would be sticking into her face, cold and unpleasant. His fingernails would be ingrained, as the fingernails of boys who owned motor-cycles always were.

'Thanks all the same,' she said.

'Come on, Jenny.'

'No, I'm busy. Honestly. I'm working at home.'

It couldn't have been pleasant, being called Chinny just because you had a jutting chin. Nicknames were horrible: there was a boy called Nut Adams and another called Wet Small and a girl called Kisses. Chinny Martin's name was Clive, but she'd never heard anyone calling him that. She felt sorry for him, standing there in his crash helmet and his special clothes. He'd probably planned it all, working it out that she'd be impressed by his gear and his motor-cycle. But of course she wasn't. *Yamaha* it said on the petrol tank of the motor-cycle, and there was a girl in a swimsuit which he had presumably stuck on to the tank himself. The girl's swimsuit was yellow and so was her hair, which was streaming out behind her, as if caught in a wind. The petrol tank was black.

'Jenny,' he said, lowering his voice so that it became almost croaks. 'Listen, Jenny—'

'Sorry.'

She began to walk away, up the village street, but he walked pushing the Yamaha.

'I love you, Jenny,' he said.

She laughed because she felt embarrassed.

'I can't bear not seeing you, Jenny.'

'Oh, well—'

'Jenny.'

They were passing the petrol-pumps, the Orchard Garage. Mr Batten was on the pavement, wiping oil from his hands with a rag. 'How's he running?' he called out to Chinny Martin, referring to the Yamaha, but Chinny Martin ignored the question.

'I think of you all the time, Jenny.'

'Oh, Clive, don't be silly.' She felt silly herself, calling him by his proper name.

'D'you like me, Jenny?'

'Of course I like you.' She smiled at him, trying to cover up the lie: she didn't particularly like him, she didn't particularly not. She just felt sorry for him, with his noticeable chin and the nickname it had given him. His father worked in the powdered-milk factory. He'd do the same: you could guess that all too easily.

'Come for a ride with me, Jenny.'

'No, honestly.'

'Why not then?'

'It's better not to start anything, Clive. Look, don't write me notes.'

'Don't you like my notes?'

'I don't want to start anything.'

'There's someone else is there, Jenny? Adam Swann? Rick Hayes?'

He sounded like a character in a television serial; he sounded sloppy and stupid.

'If you knew how I feel about you,' he said, lowering his voice even more. 'I love you like anything. It's the real thing.'

'I like you too, Clive. Only not in that way,' she hastily added.

'Wouldn't you ever? Wouldn't you even try?'

'I've told you.'

'Rick Hayes's only after sex.'

'I don't like Rick Hayes.'

'Any girl with legs on her is all he wants.'

'Yes, I know.'

'I can't concentrate on things, Jenny. I think of you the entire time.'

'I'm sorry.'

'Oh God, Jenny.'

She turned into the Mace shop just to escape. She picked up a wire basket and pretended to be looking at tins of cat food. She heard the roar of the Yamaha as her admirer rode away, and it seemed all wrong that he should have gone like that, so noisily when he was so upset.

At home she thought about the incident. It didn't in the least displease her that a boy had passionately proclaimed love for her. It even made her feel quite elated. She felt pleasantly warm when she thought about it, and the feeling bewildered her. That she, so much in love with someone else, should be moved in the very least by the immature protestations of a youth from 1B was a mystery. She even considered telling her mother about the incident, but in the end decided not to. 'Quite sprightly, she seems,' she heard her father murmuring.

'In every line of that sonnet,' Mr Tennyson said the following Monday afternoon, 'there is evidence of the richness that makes Shakespeare not just our own greatest writer but the world's as well.'

She listened, enthralled, physically pleasured by the utterance of each syllable. There was a tiredness about his boyish eyes, as if he hadn't slept. His wife had probably been bothering him, wanting him to do jobs around the house when he should have been writing sonnets of his own. She imagined him unable to sleep, lying there worrying about things, about his life. She imagined his wife like a grampus beside him, her mouth open, her upper lip as coarse as a man's.

'When forty winters shall besiege thy brow,' he said, 'And dig deep trenches in thy beauty's field.'

*Dear Jenny,* a note that morning from Chinny Martin had protested, *I just want to be with you. I just want to talk to you. Please come out with me.*

'Jenny, stay a minute,' Mr Tennyson said when the bell went. 'Your essay.'

Immediately there was tension among the girls of 1A, as if the English master had caused threads all over the classroom to become taut. Unaware the boys proceeded as they always did, throwing books into their briefcase and sauntering into the corridor. The girls lingered over anything they could think of. Jenny approached Mr Tennyson's desk.

'It's very good,' he said, opening her essay book. 'But you're getting too fond of using three little dots at the end of a sentence. The sentence should imply the dots. It's like underlining to suggest emphasis, a bad habit also.'

One by one the girls dribbled from the classroom, leaving behind them the shreds of their reluctance. Out of all of them he had chosen her: was she to be another Sarah Spence, or just some kind of stop-gap, like other girls since Sarah Spence were rumoured to have been? But as he continued to talk about her essay—called 'Belief in Ghosts'—she wondered if she'd even be a stop-gap. His fingers didn't once brush the back of her hand. His French boy's eyes didn't linger once on hers.

'I've kept you late,' he said in the end.

'That's all right, sir.'

'You will try to keep your sentences short? Your descriptions have a way of becoming too complicated.'

'I'll try, sir.'

'I really enjoyed that essay.'

He handed her the exercise book and then, without any doubt whatsoever, he smiled meaningfully into her eyes. She felt herself going hot. Her hands became clammy. She just stood there while his glance passed over her eye-shadow, over her nose and cheeks, over her mouth.

'You're very pretty,' he said.

'Thank you, sir.'

Her voice reminded her of the croak in Chinny Martin's when he'd been telling her he loved her. She tried to smile, but could not. She wanted his hand to reach out and push her gently away from him so that he could see her properly. But it didn't. He stared into her eyes again, as if endeavouring to ascertain their precise shade of blue.

'You look like a girl we had here once,' he said. 'Called Sarah Spence.'

'I remember Sarah Spence.'

'She was good at English too.'

She wanted something to happen, thunder to begin, or a torrent of rain, anything that would keep them in the class-room. She couldn't even bear the thought of walking to her desk and putting her essay book in her briefcase.

'Sarah went to Warwick University,' he said.

She nodded. She tried to smile again and this time the smile came. She said to herself that it was a brazen smile and she didn't care. She hoped it made her seem more than ever like

Sarah Spence, sophisticated and able for anything. She wondered if he said to all the girls who were stop-gaps that they looked like Sarah Spence. She didn't care. His carry-on with Sarah Spence was over and done with, he didn't even see her any more. By all accounts Sarah Spence had let him down, but never in a million years would she. She would wait for him for ever, or until the divorce came through. When he was old she would look after him.

'You'd better be getting home, Jenny.'

'I don't want to, sir.'

She continued to stand there, the exercise book in her left hand. She watched while some kind of shadow passed over his face. For a moment his eyes closed.

'Why don't you want to go?' he said.

'Because I'm in love with you, sir.'

'You mustn't be, Jenny.'

'Why not?'

'You know why not.'

'What about Sarah Spence?'

'Sarah was different.'

'I don't care how many stop-gaps you've had. I don't care. I don't love you any less.'

'What stop-gaps, Jenny?'

'The ones you made do with.'

'Made do?' He was suddenly frowning at her, his face screwed up a little. 'Made do?' he said again.

'The other girls. The ones who reminded you of her.'

'There weren't any other girls.'

'You were seen, sir—'

'Only Sarah and I were seen.'

'Your car—'

'Give a dog a bad name, Jenny. There weren't any others.'

She felt iciness inside her, somewhere in her stomach. Other girls had formed an attachment for him, as she had. Other girls had probably stood on this very spot, telling him. It was that, and the reality of Sarah Spence, that had turned him into a schoolgirls' legend. Only Sarah Spence had gone with him in his old Ford Escort to quiet lay-bys, only Sarah Spence had felt his arms around her. Why shouldn't he be seen in the buffet car of a train, alone? The weekends he'd spent away from home were probably with a sick mother.

'I'm no Casanova, Jenny.'

'I had to tell you I'm in love with you, sir. I couldn't not.'

'It's no good loving me, I'm afraid.'

'You're the nicest person I'll ever know.'

'No, I'm not, Jenny. I'm just an English teacher who took advantage of a young girl's infatuation. Shabby, people would say.'

'You're not shabby. Oh God, you're not shabby!' She heard her own voice crying out shrilly, close to tears. It astonished her. It was unbelievable that she should be so violently protesting. It was unbelievable that he should have called himself shabby.

'She had an abortion in Warwick,' he said, 'after a weekend we spent in an hotel. I let that happen, Jenny.'

'You couldn't help it.'

'Of course I could have helped it.'

Without wanting to, she imagined them in the hotel he spoke of. She imagined them having a meal, sitting opposite each other at a table, and a waiter placing plates in front of them. She imagined them in their bedroom, a grimy room with a lace curtain drawn across the lower part of the single window and a wash-basin in a corner. The bedroom had featured in a film she'd seen, and Sarah Spence was even like the actress who had played the part of a shopgirl. She stood there in her underclothes just as the shopgirl had, awkwardly waiting while he smiled his love at her. 'Then let not winter's ragged hand deface,' he whispered, 'In thee thy summer, ere thou be distilled. Oh Sarah, love.' He took the underclothes from her body, as the actor in the film had, all the time whispering sonnets.

'It was messy and horrible,' he said. 'That's how it ended, Jenny.'

'I don't care how it ended. I'd go with you anywhere. I'd go to a thousand hotels.'

'No, no, Jenny.'

'I love you terribly.'

She wept, still standing there. He got down from the stool in front of his desk and came and put his arms about her, telling her to cry. He said that tears were good, not bad. He made her sit down at a desk and then he sat down beside her.

His love affair with Sarah Spence sounded romantic, he said, and because of its romantic sheen girls fell in love with him. They fell in love with the unhappiness they sensed in him. He found it hard to stop them.

'I should move away from here,' he said, 'but I can't bring myself to do it. Because she'll always come back to see her family and whenever she does I can catch a glimpse of her.'

It was the same as she felt about him, like the glimpse that day in the International Stores. It was the same as Chinny Martin hanging about outside Harper's. And yet of course it wasn't the same as Chinny Martin. How could it possibly be? Chinny Martin was stupid and unprepossessing and ordinary.

'I'd be better to you,' she cried out in sudden desperation, unable to prevent herself. Clumsily she put a hand on his shoulder, and clumsily took it away again. 'I would wait for ever,' she said, sobbing, knowing she looked ugly.

He waited for her to calm down. He stood up and after a moment so did she. She walked with him from the classroom, down the corridor and out of the door that led to the car park.

'You can't just leave,' he said, 'a wife and four children. It was hard to explain that to Sarah. She hates me now.'

He unlocked the driver's door of the Ford Escort. He smiled at her. He said:

'There's no one else I can talk to about her. Except girls like you. You mustn't feel embarrassed in class, Jenny.'

He drove away, not offering her a lift, which he might have

done, for their direction was the same. She didn't in the least look like Sarah Spence: he'd probably said the same thing to all the others, the infatuated girls he could talk to about the girl he loved. The little scenes in the classroom, the tears, the talk: all that brought him closer to Sarah Spence. The love of a girl he didn't care about warmed him, as Chinny Martin's love had warmed her too, even though Chinny Martin was ridiculous.

She walked across the car park, imagining him driving back to his gatelodge with Sarah Spence alive again in his mind, loving her more than ever. 'Jenny,' the voice of Chinny Martin called out, coming from nowhere.

He was there, standing by his Yamaha, beside a car. She shook her head at him, and began to run. At home she would sit and eat in the kitchen with her parents, who wouldn't be any different. She would escape and lie on her bed in her small neat bedroom, longing to be where she'd never be now, beside him in his car, or on a train, or anywhere. 'Jenny,' the voice of Chinny Martin called out again, silly with his silly love.

# The Student
# from Algiers

**Rikki Ducornet**

The war has been over for only a few months, and because the French have left countless mines scattered throughout the Aurès, she cannot leave the jeep and wander, although there are many points of interest along the way, including the abandoned village of Zaouia, where she had lived, briefly, before the war. Passing near Zaouia she can see the mosque, its walls deeply scarred by machine-gun fire, its ruined minaret blackened by smoke. Zaouia where she had learned to crack melon seeds with her teeth.

That night she lies on Djamila's roof gazing at the constellations: Iouemen—"the Little Gazelles"; Chet Edoth—"the Night Maidens"; Talemt—"the She-camel." The sky moves around her like a great mouth; she is held in the mouth of the sky and expects to be swallowed whole. Later, when Djamila brings her a blanket, the two women gaze up at the sky together, talking long into the night. She tells how when in Zaouia, she had taken a lover, a student from Algiers on his way to the M'zab. She had said to him laughing, the first time they kissed: "I want you to swallow me whole!" And he, his English good, if somewhat stiff, had said: "I shall swallow you whole, but also, please, in parts."

Hearing this, Djamila roars with laughter, precipitating a shower of stars. "You Yankee!" she cries with delight, "I cannot believe you talk this way to men!" "Not any man," she says. "The one in Zaouia. The entire affair was marked by this playfulness." "Our men are not playful." Djamila is perplexed. "This man of yours, this student from Algiers, was a pearl in a sea of sand."

Before coming to Algeria she had been warned that the Algerians were haughty, stern, "madly severe." But despite the rigors and terrors of the war, her experience proves otherwise. Even perfect strangers are affable, generous. She finds a gentle kindness everywhere, a tender curiosity. Above all: a powerful sense of renewal. The war is over, the dead counted and mourned; lands are being reforested and children have returned to school. Her old friend, Djamila, has planted barley, lentils, melons, and onions; a small orchard. At dawn she awakens to the sound of turtledoves, and, moments later, when she strolls along the Wed Biskra with Djamila, they see a flock of wild ducks billing the shallow waters.

The morning he had left Zaouia, the student from Algiers said to her: "You must live in Algeria with the imagination of the dreamer." She had wanted him to say: "Come with me." Or even: "I will return to you." But he did not. She had supposed there was a woman waiting in Algiers—dark, long-boned, irreplaceable. How beautiful were the unveiled women of Algiers! Then, in the weeks and months after his departure she had lived a dream of such wanting that when Hugo had joined her group at the diggings near Erg Tekchouli, he had appeared to her like an oasis hazy with the promise of water.

The night she had accepted Hugo, and as she slept beside him, she dreamed that she was walking naked and alone down the corridors of a dark hotel. Suddenly the student from Algiers was standing before her, gazing at her with scorn. Points of fire, his eyes burned her body with the terrible, the precise heat of an incandescent cigarette. She awakened in a place she did not recognize, nor did she recognize the man beside her, the one she had chosen, the one she did not love.

Illumined by a thin blade of moonlight, a white scorpion was climbing the wall. She was in her own tent somewhere off the camel *piste* to In Salah. In the dark Hugo seemed far too large to be human. He lay beside her like a thing of necromantic clay she had conjured from weakness or folly. And yet a few hours earlier, Hugo had covered her body with kisses and held her naked feet in his hands. What had she been thinking of? But then, as if to prove she was in love and madly, she pressed against him, murmuring his name. Had the student from Algiers been standing in the shadows, he would have been fooled.

This morning on her way to the M'zab, her humiliation and rage are such she is tempted to tear her hair, tear the flesh of her face and neck as she has seen the women of the desert do in times of acute distress. Her injured, ill-used heart is become so wasted as to cause her constant pain—the dull ache of sorrow and something like dread. Because she has come to understand that if the student from Algiers never told her his name, had left without an address or a word, it is because he was somehow actively engaged in the insurrection which, during her time in Zaouia, had evolved into a full-scale revolutionary war.

Could she rip into her chest now and pull her heart out by the roots it would not be recognizable. She describes her heart to herself as she muses over a scarlet land that, in the morning sun, appears to bleed: a tiny shell, a dead shell black as soot, heavy as gravity, and pumping a dirty water.

Here in the Sahara she can become a perfume, a melody, pure thought. She can become an erasure, silence. Yes, she can become an absence, the air in suspension between two grains of sand. All this as a way out, as a way of excising the humiliation of having chosen Hugo. As a way of excising the terrible, the imperious longing for the one in Zaouia who had vanished so suddenly she had spent the next set of days standing in a sand-laden wind, watching the land weather away.

Now on her way south, the sun spills over the road like a hot tide and the red desert metamorphoses into a mirror reflection of a blond sky, transparent, almost ethereal. How she loves this mutable land, the hours spent puzzling over the fragments of a vanished world, fragments of an insufficient alphabet: ostrich-shell beads, implements of quartzitic sandstone, of clear chalcedony, moss agate, fine jasper. Red and yellow ochre. Ivory needles and combs. Shells charred by fire. Things she takes pleasure in recording in pencil or ink on large sheets of heavy paper.

Before the war, at a site near Erg Tekchouli, she had found a pearl, the largest she had ever seen and the most beautifully worked. A week later, visiting a Tuareg encampment, she saw virtually the same bead hanging from the lovely neck of a living girl. With gravity the girl had offered her a bowl of milk and all at once the dust of the excavations had become a measurement of the real. Ever after when she found a bead of ostrich shell or a glass pearl, she saw the girl's intent face and tasted milk.

The projects she and Hugo worked on together were sponsored by the museum of a prestigious American university. But it seemed to her that the artifacts they found belonged to the desert, not to them. That having documented the sites they should return everything. Hugo pointed out that the university paid them for more than knowledge; the university wanted artifacts, and her sentimentalism would cost them both a job. She fell silent but continued brooding: *Every single thing we find is a potency, has meaning.* The glass pearl the girl wore was blue—the inimitable blue of Heaven; was white—the white of the molar of the healthy servant girl; was gray—the color of the turtledove, of constancy.

For a few months there was another woman involved in the project—Monica, so blond, so pale she had a tendency to vanish like a lizard in the sand. Early on Hugo began to implore her, whenever he made love to her, to seduce Monica, to bring her into their bed. She refused, not because she loved him but, perhaps, because she did not love him enough. (Although she supposed that had she loved him enough, the thought of sharing him would have been unbearable; the thought of watching him enter the body of another, unbearable; unbearable too, Monica's eyes watching them.) Monica, flamboyant, a healthy animal, her body the color of sand, deserved better.

When she thinks of Hugo, she feels ashamed for him and for herself. What is it the French say? *Hélas, Hélas!* And the Arabs? *Ya! Allah!* (The times, she knows, were humiliating for them all.) This morning as she left Biskra, Djamila had said: "It is time for us all to shed our skins." Djamila was referring to a man lost to the war.

After the museum project was canceled she returned to America with Hugo because by then she feared that if she left him he would die. She began to think of herself as Hugo's "keeper" as though he were a beast—and this even after she was well aware that he lived in a cage of his own making. But then one morning she awoke with the thought: *I have been skinned alive.* And: *I have allowed myself to be peeled, peeled and eaten like a piece of fruit.* At least she had recognized that Hugo was her cage, the cage of her own taking. She was the one kept.

*Eaten like a piece of fruit.* The sensuality of this image sends her thoughts winging back to the student from Algiers. Her love for him is like a continuous water, a true desert where everything glistens. One by one she recalls their nights of red clay, their red nights, those generous nights when endearments murmured unceasingly like water.

She ponders this: When the student from Algiers had taken her flesh in his mouth, he had healed her of a wound she had not known she had. The night she had taken Hugo into her tent, that wound had reopened.

She is now approaching the white cliffs and green palms of Berriane, an oasis of the M'zab. A golden eagle accompanies her; flying high he shines in the late afternoon sun like molten metal. Somewhere in the M'zab she hopes to find her lover's traces. She sees the eagle as an auspicious sign.

Each morning in Berriane, Belaid brings her a bowl of fresh camel milk and a wheel of unleavened bread. He brings her a basket of dates, pomegranates, figs. Sometimes he brings her *tikomaren*—the dried cheese of the Tuaregs of the Ahaggar—because she told him how, before the war on her travels in that region, she had come to love it "like gnawing stones!" "And glass!" Belaid had laughed. "You need a gizzard to digest in the desert!"

She pays him every day, the coins sewn to a piece of heavy drawing paper, beneath a sketch of the palms or a clump of tamarisks, the distant mountains, the ravine. Or a portrait, or the palms swarming with turtledoves, or children harvesting quinces. This time her project is a book, the visions of a dreamer, the dreamer of the Sahara she has become. She wants to capture it all, to capture the shape of time, to offer it lovingly to the one who has vanished, one for whom love had been a living water.

Today when Belaid comes she is sweeping sand from the guesthouse rooms and from the little courtyard where they will drink tea together and delight in one another's conversation. In his youth, Belaid had been an itinerant singer and now if his voice is broken, still he has not lost his gifts entirely. A handsome man, close to eighty, he has already confided, not without pride, that as he had "floated" from the M'zab to the Ahaggar, he had fathered minstrels, magicians, acrobats, a skilled weaver, and warriors: two of his sons had gone north to fight the French in the Aurès.

Knowing how well the women of the Sahara are watched, she had expressed surprise. "Entertainers are like fish in water," Belaid explained. "We winnow our way into this and that." Clapping his hands he burst into song:

*The Sahara is a Palace of Trespass,*
*The gate to a world where nothing is fixed,*
*Where everything scatters like swallows and swifts,*
*Where everything scatters like sand.*
*Life flows through the fingers like water; Love bruises the fingers*
*like sand.*

Belaid learned to speak the dialects of the women he loved, the children he fathered: *zenaga, hassania, tamachek, azeir* . . . a precious capacity he offered to the FLN when news of the insurrection had reached Berriane. "I, my sons, and my daughters spun a web of words," he told her, "from Biskra to Tassili." He continued: "I could never carry a gun, but in my way I fought the French, the same French who, when I was a little boy, measured the heads of everyone in Berriane, even the heads of the women: my mother's and sisters' and aunts'. They fingered us like insects, like rotten fruit. Those fingers left a mark at my temple, here—" He had turned his head to show her a small, red mole. "After they left we scrubbed our bodies with stones. My mother said: 'In the entire universe there is not enough water to wash away the shame.' This I will never forget."

Later, when a French soldier cut the breasts from a girl who had been caught taking water to the rebels, Belaid was not surprised. And when the villagers of Zaouia were lined up against the wall of the mosque, "lined up like empty bottles and shot," no, he had not been surprised. And when the *paras* had brought out the *gigène* and pushed a live wire into his most private place, he had not been surprised and he had not talked, either.

Belaid is now before her, smiling what can only be called a complicitous smile. And this because they have shared so much sadness, so much laughter this past week, told one another so many stories. He bows his head and lifts his hands briefly in greeting:

"*Le salut sur vous!*"

"*Sur vows le salut!*"

Today he has brought her gifts: a lettuce from his own garden and freshly fried fritters to go with their morning tea. His granddaughter has made the fritters. It is nine o'clock. Together they will eat the fritters and talk. Perhaps they will talk for so long they will get hungry again and she will get up to fetch dates from the kitchen, and milk. They will sit in the shade of the ancient tamarisk on a palm mat so clean a baby could be born there, and Belaid will sing and they will exchange the stories of their lives, which, now that they have begun to tell them, could prove to be without end.

Belaid will never allow her to make the tea. He has his own eccentric English teapot he keeps polished to a high shine and carries about in a box. The guesthouse's little kerosene stove is shining brightly too. When he sees it Belaid cries: "There is little to occupy you here!" "Baba!" she scolds him. "You've seen my drawings! You know how busy

I am!" "Yes, I do know. Beautiful drawings. You are an artist, you—the unveiled American woman who draws Algerian pictures with Italian pencils on French paper and who goes about dressed in pantaloons—"

"I offend you!"

"No! Not at all. I am a free thinker. There are not many free thinkers here."

"Nor where I come from."

"But, I am wondering . . ."

"Yes? I give you permission, Baba, to wonder out loud."

"Why she is alone, the lady in pantaloons. She is too pretty to be alone—you will excuse an old man for speaking the truth. Again and again I ask myself *Why is she not married?*"

"Because I am divorced." Suddenly giddy she adds, laughing: "Three times I said: 'I divorce thee.'"

"Is this possible? Such a thing!" Belaid widens his eyes in mock astonishment. "Allah be praised," he says, "that American women can divorce so easily, like Tuaregs."

"But *I am* a Tuareg! Baba—you've seen me on a camel. You've seen me eat *tikomaren* and *kessra*!"

He roars with laughter:

"The Tuaregs may know how to divorce, but they don't know how to eat!"

"Those who know how to divorce know how to eat!"

"You are a fast talker," he complains, or pretends to. "Put a woman in pantaloons and she'll talk off a man's ears!" Belaid begins to sing:

*I knew such a one in Metlili*
*Who lost both his ears in this manner.*
*His wife bit off his nose next*
*And tied up his tongue—*
*He's as smooth as an egg, now*
*And a stammerer.*

"Baba," she says, "I truly wish you were several decades younger."

"*Ya! Allah!*" He pours her a second cup of tea. "*Hélas, hélas, jolie dame.*"

Burning hot the tea is her only luxury and it warms her to the marrow. The tea, the friendship with Belaid, his stories, the songs he sings in a voice that seems to have been hammered out of a thin sheet of brass. An ancient voice that bent by time has traces of verdigris pocking its bright surface.

The landscape, too, is a luxury. Its silence is wonderful, the tangible proof that when Allah made the world he paused between two spoken words. And what if Allah had spoken too quickly? Would those words have collided causing a conflagration? As it was the pause was almost too brief. During the middle of the day it is so hot nothing moves. This is when she chooses the coolest room in the guesthouse, tiled and dark, to sit as still as a stone, her mind suspended in her skull like the egg of a bird that hatches only after a thousand years' incubation. Her mind a stone at the bottom of a deep pool, her thoughts water.

"What are you thinking? You are very far away!"

"I am thinking I want to hear you sing again, Baba, even though—pardon me telling an old man the truth—your voice is like a brass tray pelted with sand."

"Ah, I am fortunate to sing at all. I am fortunate the French did not force me to swallow the wire as they did my friend Abdelaziz. When he cried out, 'Pity! Pity for God's sake!' the *paras* replied: 'No pity for Arabs.'"

She fears she has hurt him and lowers her eyes. For a time they sip their tea in silence. But then Belaid begins to sing. He sings a wordless melody that gently fingers her heart, a thrilling melody that causes her to close her eyes in rapture. Almost before she is aware of it the words are winging, words in classical Arabic, very unlike Belaid's own dialect:

*If one believes Herodotus*
*Arabia was once green with palms*
*The only place in the universe*
*Where cassia flourished, incense and myrrh*
*Laudanum and cinnamon.*

*Theophrastus wrote that incense and myrrh*
*Grew side by side and Pliny proposed*
*Another impossibility. He said*
*These disparate things*
*Were wept by the same tree.*

*The men who harvested the sacred groves*
*Were forbidden to touch their wives . . .*
*But only for the season of the harvest.*
*Incense fills the hand like a woman's breast.*
*Like love it is ephemeral.*

*Myrrh, too, weeps milk*
*Like the stars its fruit are of unequal size.*
*Myrrh, too, is gathered by abstentious men*
*Then it is taken to a temple*
*The most sacred in Saba.*

*A part of the gum is given to the sun:*
*A gift for that most volatile body, the sun.*

As he sings, the world dissolves, and when the song is over it is midday; they are embraced by silence. At last she sighs deeply and says, "Baba. Such a wonderful song! An ancient song—or so it seems—and a learned song. How did you come by it?"

"The song is the invention of one who came through here at the outset of the war. One who told us where to dig our new wells. Three wells so deep they touch the navel of the world. And water so fresh, so pure—although it is—he said it—an ancient water. Salt everywhere" —Belaid gestures with his arms—"but not where he told us to dig."

She follows his gaze out across the fractured, riddled land

of the M'zab, little hills of salt glittering on the surface for miles. Belaid points east—

"Further there is a purple salt." She tells him that she would very much like to have some of this salt. "I will take you there," Belaid tells her, "and also to Recheg, where there is chalcedony scattered over the ground. And to Djelfa, where there are many shells turned to stone. And to the place where the golden eagle makes his nest. And to the place where I once found a needle made from the bone of a bird."

"Thank you. I would very much like to visit these places with you, Baba." She goes to the kitchen for milk and dates, two bowls, two spoons. "The song," she says when she returns. "Where did the well-digger learn it?

Did it come from the Gulf, perhaps? Was it originally Greek?"

"It was a song of his invention. He made up songs to 'animate the hours.' These are his words. He was a student of geography and geology, but also of history and politics and literature . . . in other words: a true scholar. A young man came all this way from Algiers. He is the one who told us of the insurrection."

"Here! From Algiers! How extraordinary." She rises and excitedly begins to pace. "Because, you see, I am looking for someone I knew in Zaouia in the early months of the war. He was on his way south—somewhere in the M'zab." Her breath catches: "Baba—I never knew his name. So how can I possibly find him? And then . . . I am fearful. Because I suppose he was a member of the FLN. And that this is why he could not tell me his name. Or why he was going south. Was the one who came here a member of the FLN?"

Belaid is still. He is looking into his cup as though a world were contained there.

"Baba?" She walks to him and crouches down. "Could it be the same man?" Gently she touches his sleeve. "Can you tell me his name?"

The old man continues to stare into his cup. She sees a bright tear fall from his face, making the sound of one drop of rain.

"His name was Messali," he whispers.

"Messali!" Her heart is leaping. "Messali."

"Achmed. His name was Achmed."

"Baba," she says. "I do not understand."

"His name was Abdallah." Belaid continues, his voice rising. "His name was Sayyid. His name was Mafoul. His name was Abdelaziz. He was held for a month in El-Biar. He was tortured every day for a month in El-Biar. . . ."

Trembling, she gently tugs at his sleeve. His eyes are welling over, the tears flooding his face.

"Her name was Lâlia," he says softly. "Her name was Jatchi. Her name was Shwa'wish. . . ." And Belaid screams, a terrible scream that rending the air causes all the dogs of Berriane to awaken from their midday slumber and to howl. She leans over and holds him in her arms tenderly as she would a father, a brother, a lover, a son. Rocking back and forth and speaking softly as if in prayer, Belaid whispers:

"These are the names, honored friend, I did not say aloud. I held them in my heart and was silent, even though they put the wire deep into my body. And these are the ones who died in pain despite my silence. If I survived it is only because they thought me too old to kill."

That night she bathes her body slowly. She fills a large bowl with water. She rubs every inch of her body with a rough cloth. She bathes every inch of her body with water. She wonders if there will ever be enough water.

# The Most Beautiful Woman in Town

Charles Bukowski

Cass was the youngest and most beautiful of 5 sisters. Cass was the most beautiful girl in town. ½ Indian with a supple and strange body, a snake-like and fiery body with eyes to go with it. Cass was fluid moving fire. She was like a spirit stuck into a form that would not hold her. Her hair was black and long and silken and moved and whirled about as did her body. Her spirit was either very high or very low. There was no in between for Cass. Some said she was crazy. The dull ones said that. The dull ones would never understand Cass. To the men she simply seemed a sex machine and they didn't care whether she was crazy or not. And Cass danced and flirted, kissed the men, but except for an instance or two, when it came time to make it with Cass, Cass had somehow slipped away, eluded the men.

Her sisters accused her of misusing her beauty, of not using her mind enough, but Cass had mind and spirit; she painted, she danced, she sang, she made things of clay, and when people were hurt either in the spirit or the flesh, Cass felt a deep grieving for them. Her mind was simply different; her mind was simply not practical. Her sisters were jealous of her because she attracted their men, and they were angry because they felt she didn't make the best use of them. She had a habit of being kind to the uglier ones; the so-called handsome men revolted her— "No guts," she said, "no zap. They are riding on their perfect little earlobes and their well-shaped nostrils … All surface and no insides . . ." She had a temper that came close to insanity; she had a temper that some called insanity.

Her father had died of alcohol and her mother had run off leaving the girls alone. The girls went to a relative who placed them in a convent. The convent had been an unhappy place, more for Cass than the sisters. The girls were jealous of Cass and Cass fought most of them. She had razor marks all along her left arm from defending herself in two fights. There was also a permanent scar along the left cheek but the scar rather than lessening her beauty only seemed to highlight it.

I met her at the West End Bar several nights after her release from the convent. Being youngest, she was the last of the sisters to be released. She simply came in and sat next to me. I was probably the ugliest man in town and this might have had something to do with it.

"Drink?" I asked.

"Sure, why not?"

I don't suppose there was anything unusual in our conversation that night, it was simply in the feeling Cass gave. She had chosen me and it was as simple as that. No pressure. She liked her drinks and had a great number of them. She didn't seem quite of age but they served her anyhow. Perhaps she had a forged i.d., I don't know. Anyhow, each time she came back from the restroom and sat down next to me, I did feel some pride. She was not only the most beautiful woman in town but also one of the most beautiful I had ever seen. I placed my arm about her waist and kissed her once.

"Do you think I'm pretty?" she asked.

"Yes, of course, but there's something else ... there's more than your looks . . ."

"People are always accusing me of being pretty. Do you really think I'm pretty?"

"Pretty isn't the word, it hardly does you fair."

Cass reached into her handbag. I thought she was reaching for her handkerchief. She came out with a long hatpin. Before I could stop her she had run this long hat pin through her nose, sideways, just above the nostrils. I felt disgust and horror.

She looked at me and laughed, "Now do you think me pretty? What do you think now, man?"

I pulled the hatpin out and held my handkerchief over the bleeding. Several people, including the bartender, had seen the act. The bartender came down:

"Look," he said to Cass, "you act up again and you're out. We don't need your dramatics here."

"Oh, fuck you, man!" she said.

"Better keep her straight," the bartender said to me.

"She'll be all right," I said.

"It's my nose," said Cass, "I can do what I want with my nose."

"No," I said, "it hurts me."

"You mean it hurts you when I stick a pin in my nose?"

"Yes, it does. I mean it."

"All right, I won't do it again. Cheer up."

She kissed me, rather grinning through the kiss and holding the handkerchief to her nose. We left for my place at closing time. I had some beer and we sat there talking. It was then that I got the perception of her as a person full of kindness and caring. She gave herself away without knowing it. At the same time she would leap back into areas of wildness and incoherence. Schitzi. A beautiful and spiritual *schitzi*. Perhaps some man, something, would ruin her forever. I hoped that it wouldn't be me.

We went to bed and after I turned out the lights Cass asked me, "When do you want it? Now or in the morning?"

"In the morning," I said and turned my back.

In the morning I got up and made a couple of coffees, brought her one in bed.

She laughed. "You're the first man I've met who has turned it down at night."

"It's o.k.," I said, "we needn't do it at all."

"No, wait, I want to now. Let me freshen up a bit."

Cass went to the bathroom. She came out shortly, looking quite wonderful, her long black hair glistening, her eyes and lips glistening, *her* glistening... She displayed her body calmly, as a good thing. She got under the sheet.

"Come on, lover man."

I got on in.

She kissed with abandon but without haste. I let my hands run over her body, through her hair. I mounted. It was hot, and tight. I began to stroke slowly, wanting to make it last. Her eyes looked directly into mine.

"What's your name?" I asked.

"What the hell difference does it make?" she asked.

I laughed and went on ahead. Afterwards she dressed and I drove her back to the bar but she was difficult to forget. I wasn't working and I slept until 2 p.m. then got up and read the paper. I was in the bathtub when she came in with a large leaf—an elephant ear.

"I knew you'd be in the bathtub," she said, "so I brought you something to cover that thing with, nature boy."

She threw the elephant leaf down on me in the bathtub.

"How did you know I'd be in the tub?"

"I knew."

Almost everyday Cass arrived when I was in the tub. The times were different but she seldom missed, and there was the elephant leaf. And then we'd make love.

One or two nights she phoned and I had to bail her out of jail for drunkenness and fighting.

"These sons of bitches," she said, "just because they buy you a few drinks they think they can get into your pants."

"Once you accept a drink you create your own trouble."

"I thought they were interested in me, not just my body."

"I'm interested in you *and* your body. I doubt, though, that most men can see beyond your body."

I left town for 6 months, bummed around, came back. I had never forgotten Cass, but we'd had some type of argument and I felt like moving on anyhow, and when I got back I figured she'd be gone, but I had been sitting in the West End Bar about 30 minutes when she walked in and sat down next to me.

"Well, bastard, I see you've come back."

I ordered her a drink. Then I looked at her. She had on a high-necked dress. I had never seen her in one of those. And under each eye, driven in, were 2 pins with glass heads. All you could see were the glass heads of the pins, but the pins were driven down into her face.

"God damn you, still trying to destroy your beauty, eh?"

"No, it's the *fad*, you fool."

"You're crazy.

"I've missed you," she said.

"Is there anybody else?"

"No, there isn't anybody else. Just you. But I'm hustling. It costs ten bucks. But you get it free."

"Pull those pins out."

"No, it's the fad."

"It's making me very unhappy."

"Are you sure?"

"Hell yes, I'm sure."

Cass slowly pulled the pins out and placed them in her purse.

"Why do you haggle your beauty?" I asked. "Why don't you just live with it?"

"Because people think it's all I have. Beauty is nothing, beauty won't stay. You don't know how lucky you are to be ugly, because if people like you then you know it's for something else."

"O.k.," I said, "I'm lucky."

"I don't mean you're ugly. People just think you're ugly. You have a fascinating face."

"Thanks."

We had another drink.

"What are you doing?" she asked.

"Nothing. I can't get on to anything. No interest."

"Me neither. If you were a woman you could hustle."

"I don't think I'd want to make that close a contact with so many strangers. It's wearing."

"You're right, it's wearing, everything is wearing."

We left together. People still stared at Cass on the streets. She was still a beautiful woman, perhaps more beautiful than ever.

We made it to my place and I opened a bottle of wine and we talked. With Cass and I, the talk always came easy. She talked a while and I would listen and then I would talk. Our conversation simply went along without strain. We seemed to discover secrets together. When we discovered a good one Cass would laugh that laugh—only the way she could. It was like joy out of fire. Through the talking we kissed and moved closer together. We became quite heated and decided to go to bed. It was then Cass took off her high-necked dress and I saw it—the ugly jagged scar across her throat. It was large and thick.

"God damn you, woman," I said from the bed, "god damn you, what have you done?"

"I tried it with a broken bottle one night. Don't you like me anymore? Am I still beautiful?"

I pulled her down on the bed and kissed her. She pushed away and laughed, "Some men pay me that ten and then I undress and they don't want to do it. I keep the ten. It's very funny."

"Yes," I said, "I can't stop laughing … Cass, bitch, I love you … stop destroying yourself; you're the most alive woman I've ever met."

We kissed again. Cass was crying without sound. I could feel the tears. That long black hair lay behind me like a flag of death. We enjoined and made slow and sombre and wonderful love.

In the morning Cass was up making breakfast. She seemed quite calm and happy. She was singing. I stayed in bed and enjoyed her happiness. Finally she came over and shook me, "Up, bastard! Throw some cold water on your face and pecker and come enjoy the feast!"

I drove her to the beach that day. It was a weekday and not yet summer so things were splendidly deserted. Beach bums in rags slept on the lawns above the sand. Others sat on stone benches sharing a lone bottle. The gulls whirled about, mindless yet distracted. Old ladies in their 70's and 80's sat on the benches and discussed selling real estate left behind by husbands long ago killed by the pace and stupidity of survival. For it all, there was peace in the air and we walked about and stretched on the lawns and didn't say much. It simply felt good being together. I bought a couple of sandwiches, some chips and drinks and we sat on the sand eating. Then I held Cass and we slept together about an hour. It was somehow better than love-making. There was a flowing together without tension. When we awakened we drove back to my place and I cooked a dinner. After dinner I suggested to Cass that we shack together. She waited a long time, looking at me, then she slowly said, "No." I drove her back to the bar, bought her a drink and walked out. I found a job as a packer in a factory the next day and the rest of the week went to working. I was too tired to get about much but that Friday night I did get to the West End Bar. I sat and waited for Cass. Hours went by. After I was fairly drunk the bartender said to me, "I'm sorry about your girl friend."

"What is it?" I asked.

"I'm sorry. Didn't you know?"

"No."

"Suicide. She was buried yesterday."

"Buried?" I asked. It seemed as if she would walk through the doorway at any moment. How could she be gone?

"Her sisters buried her."

"A suicide? Mind telling me how?"

"She cut her throat."

"I see. Give me another drink."

I drank until closing time. Cass the most beautiful of 5 sisters, the most beautiful in town. I managed to drive to my place and I kept thinking, I should have *insisted* she stay with me instead of accepting that "no." Everything about her had indicated that she had cared. I had simply been too offhand about it, lazy, too unconcerned. I deserved my death and hers. I was a dog. No, why blame the dogs? I got up and found a bottle of wine and drank from it heavily. Cass the most beautiful girl in town was dead at 20.

Outside somebody honked their automobile horn. They were very loud and persistent. I set the bottle down and screamed out: "GOD DAMN YOU, YOU SON OF A BITCH, SHUT UP!"

The night kept coming on in and there was nothing I could do.

# Doc's Story

John Edgar Wideman

He thinks of her small, white hands, blue veined, gaunt, awkwardly knuckled. He'd teased her about the smallness of her hands, hers lost in the shadow of his when they pressed them together palm to palm to measure. The heavy drops of color on her nails barely reached the middle joints of his fingers. He'd teased her about her dwarf's hands but he'd also said to her one night when the wind was rattling the windows of the apartment on Cedar and they lay listening and shivering though it was summer on the brass bed she'd found in a junk store on Haverford Avenue, near the Woolworth's five-and-dime they'd picketed for two years, that God made little things closer to perfect than he ever made big things. Small, compact women like her could be perfectly formed, proportioned, and he'd smiled out loud running his hand up and down the just-right fine lines of her body, celebrating how good she felt to him.

She'd left him in May, when the shadows and green of the park had started to deepen. Hanging out, becoming a regular at the basketball court across the street in Regent Park was how he'd coped. No questions asked. Just the circle of stories. If you didn't want to miss anything good you came early and stayed late. He learned to wait, be patient. Long hours waiting were not time lost but time doing nothing because there was nothing better to do. Basking in sunshine on a stone bench, too beat to play any longer, nowhere to go but an empty apartment, he'd watch the afternoon traffic in Regent Park, dog strollers, baby carriages, winos, kids, gays, students with blankets they'd spread out on the grassy banks of the hollow and books they'd pretend to read, the black men from the neighborhood who'd search the park for bra-less young mothers and white girls on blankets who didn't care or didn't know any better than to sit with their crotches exposed. When he'd sit for hours like that, cooking like that, he'd feel himself empty out, see himself seep away and hover in the air, a fine mist, a little, flattened-out gray cloud of something wavering in the heat, a presence as visible as the steam on the window as he stares for hours at winter.

He's waiting for summer. For the guys to begin gathering on the court again. They'll sit in the shade with their backs against the Cyclone fencing or lean on cars parked at the roller-coaster curb or lounge in the sun on low, stone benches catty-corner from the basketball court. Some older ones still drink wine, but most everybody cools out on reefer, when there's reefer passed along, while they bullshit and wait for winners. He collects the stories they tell. He needs a story now. The right one now to get him through this long winter because she's gone and won't leave him alone.

In summer fine grit hangs in the air. Five minutes on the court and you're coughing. City dirt and park dust blowing off bald patches from which green is long gone, and deadly ash blowing over from New Jersey. You can taste it some days, bitter in your spit. Chunks pepper your skin, burn your eyes. Early fall while it's still warm enough to run outdoors the worst time of all. Leaves pile up against the fence, higher and higher, piles that explode and jitterbug across the court in the middle of a game, then sweep up again, slamming back where they blew from. After a while the leaves are ground into coarse, choking powder. You eat leaf trying to get in a little hoop before the weather turns, before those days when nobody's home from work yet but it's dark already and too cold to run again till spring. Fall's the only time sweet syrupy wine beats reefer. Ripple, Manischewitz, Taylor's Tawny Port coat your throat. He takes a hit when the jug comes round. He licks the sweetness from his lips, listens for his favorite stories one more time before everybody gives it up till next season.

His favorite stories made him giggle, and laugh and hug the others, like they hugged him when a story got so good nobody's legs could hold them up. Some stories got under his skin in peculiar ways. Some he liked to hear because they made the one performing them do crazy stuff with his voice and body. He learned to be patient, learned his favorites would be repeated, get a turn just like he got a turn on the joints and wine bottles circulating the edges of the court.

Of all the stories, the one about Doc had bothered him most. Its orbit was unpredictable. Twice in one week, then only once more last summer. He'd only heard Doc's story three times, but that was enough to establish Doc behind and between the words of all the other stories. In a strange way Doc presided over the court. You didn't need to mention him. He was just there. Regent Park stories began with Doc and ended with Doc and everything in between was preparation, proof the circle was unbroken.

They say Doc lived on Regent Square, one of the streets like Cedar, dead-ending at the park. On the hottest afternoons the guys from the court would head for Doc's stoop. Jars of ice water, the good feeling and good talk they'd share in the shade of Doc's little front yard was what drew them. Sometimes they'd spray Doc's hose on one another. Get drenched like when they were kids and the city used to turn on fire hydrants in the summer. Some of Doc's neighbors would give them dirty looks. Didn't like a whole bunch of loud, sweaty, half-naked niggers backed up in their nice street where Doc was the only colored on the block. They say Doc didn't care. He was just out there like everybody else having a good time.

Doc had played at the University. Same one where Doc

taught for a while. They say Doc used to laugh when white people asked him if he was in the Athletic Department. No reason for niggers to be at the University if they weren't playing ball or coaching ball. At least that's what white people thought, and since they thought that way, that's the way it was. Never more than a sprinkle of black faces in the white sea of the University. Doc used to laugh till the joke got old. People freedom-marching and freedom-dying, Doc said, but some dumb stuff never changed.

He first heard Doc's story late one day, after the yellow streetlights had popped on. Pooner was finishing the one about gang warring in North Philly: Yeah. They sure nuff lynched this dude they caught on their turf. Hung him up on the goddamn poles behind the backboard. Little kids found the sucker in the morning with his tongue all black and shit down his legs, and the cops had to come cut him down. Worst part is them little kids finding a dead body swinging up there. Kids don't be needing to find nothing like that. But those North Philly gangs don't play. They don't even let the dead rest in peace. Run in a funeral parlor and fuck up the funeral. Dumping over the casket and tearing up the flowers. Scaring people and turning the joint out. It's some mean shit. But them gangs don't play. They kill you they ain't finished yet. Mess with your people, your house, your sorry-ass dead body to get even. Pooner finished telling it and he looked round at the fellows and people were shaking their heads and then there was a chorus of You got that right, man. It's a bitch

out there, man. Them niggers crazy, boy, and Pooner holds
out his hand and somebody passes the joint. Pooner pinches
it in two fingers and takes a deep drag. Everybody knows he's
finished, it's somebody else's turn.

One of the fellows says, I wonder what happened to old
Doc. I always be thinking about Doc, wondering where the
cat is, what he be doing now …

Don't nobody know why Doc's eyes start to going bad. It
just happen. Doc never even wore glasses. Eyes good as anybody's far as anybody knew till one day he come round he got
goggles on. Like Kareem. And people kinda joking, you know.
Doc got him some goggles. Watch out, youall. Doc be sky-
hooking youall to death today. Funning, you know. Cause
Doc like to joke and play. Doc one the fellas like I said, so
when he come round in goggles he subject to some teasing
and one another thing like that cause nobody thought nothing serious wrong. Doc's eyes just as good as yours or mine,
far as anybody knew.

Doc been playing all his life. That's why you could stand
him on the foul line and point him at the hoop and more times
than not, Doc could sink it. See he be remembering.

His muscles know just what to do. You get his feet aimed
right, line him up so he's on target, and Doc would swish one
for you. Was a game kinda. Sometimes you get a sucker and
Doc win you some money. Swish. Then the cat lost the dough
start crying. He ain't blind. Can't no blind man shoot no pill.
Is you really blind, brother? You niggers trying to steal my

money, trying to play me for a fool. When a dude start crying the blues like that Doc wouldn't like it. He'd walk away. Wouldn't answer.

Leave the man lone. You lost fair and square. Doc made the basket so shut up and pay up, chump.

Doc practiced. Remember how you'd hear him out here at night when people sleeping. It's dark but what dark mean to Doc? Blacker than the rentman's heart but don't make no nevermind to Doc, he be steady shooting fouls. Always be somebody out there to chase the ball and throw it back. But shit, man. When Doc into his rhythm, didn't need nobody chase the ball. Ball be swishing with that good backspin, that good arch bring it back blip, blip, blip, three bounces and it's coming right back to Doc's hands like he got a string on the pill. Spooky if you didn't know Doc or know about foul shooting and understand when you got your shit together don't matter if you blindfolded. You put the motherfucker up and you know it's spozed to come running back just like a dog with a stick in his mouth.

Doc always be hanging at the court. Blind as wood but you couldn't fool Doc. Eyes in his ears. Know you by your walk. He could tell if you wearing new sneaks, tell you if your old ones is laced or not. Know you by your breath. The holes you make in the air when you jump. Doc was hip to who fucking who and who was getting fucked. Who could play ball and who was jiving. Doc use to be out here every weekend, steady rapping with the fellows and doing his foul-shot thing between games. Every once in a while somebody tease him, Hey, Doc. You want to run winners next go? Doc laugh and say, No, Dupree ... I'm tired today, Dupree. Besides which you ain't been on a winning team in a week have you, Du? And everybody laugh. You know, just funning cause Doc one the fellas.

But one Sunday the shit got stone serious. Sunday I'm telling youall about, the action was real nice. If you wasn't ready, get back cause the brothers was cooking. Sixteen points, rise and fly. Next. Who got next? ... Come on out here and take your ass kicking. One them good days when it's hot and everybody's juices is high and you feel you could play till next week. One them kind of days and a run's just over. Doc gets up and he goes with Billy Moon to the foul line. Fellas hanging under the basket for the rebound. Ain't hardly gon be a rebound Doc get hisself lined up right. But see, when the ball drop through the net you want to be the one grab it and throw it back to Billy. You want to be out there part of Doc shooting fouls just like you want to run when the running's good.

Doc bounce the ball, one, two, three times like he does. Then he raise it. Sift it in his fingers. You know he's a ball-player, a shooter already way the ball spin in them long fingers way he raises it and cocks his wrist. You know Doc can't see a damn thing through his sunglasses but swear to God you'd think he was looking at the hoop way he study and measure. Then he shoots and ain't a sound in whole Johnson.

Seems like everybody's heart stops. Everybody's breath behind that ball pushing it and steadying it so it drops through clean as new money.

But that Sunday something went wrong. Couldna been wind cause wasn't no wind. I was there. I know. Maybe Doc had playing on his mind. Couldn't help have playing on his mind cause it was one those days wasn't nothing better to do in the world than play. Whatever it was, soon as the ball left his hands, you could see Doc was missing, missing real bad. Way short and way off to the left. Might hit the backboard if everybody blew on it real hard.

A young boy, one them skinny, jumping jack young boys got pogo sticks for legs, one them kids go up and don't come back down till they ready, he was standing on the left side the lane and leap up all the sudden catch the pill out the air and jams it through. Blam. A monster dunk and everybody break out in Goddamn. Do it, Sky, and Did you see that nigger get up? People slapping five and all that mess. Then Sky, the young boy they call Sky, grinning like a Chessy cat and strutting out with the ball squeezed in one hand to give it to Doc. In his glory. Grinning and strutting.

Gave you a little help, Doc.

Didn't ask for no help, Sky. Why'd you fuck with my shot, Sky?

Well, up jumped the Devil. The joint gets real quiet again real quick. Doc ain't cracked smile the first. He ain't playing.

Sorry, Doc. Didn't mean no harm, Doc.

You must think I'm some kind of chump fucking with my shot that way.

People start to feeling bad. Doc is steady getting on Sky's case. Sky just a young, light-in-the-ass kid. Jump to the moon but he's just a silly kid. Don't mean no harm. He just out there like everybody else trying to do his thing. No harm in Sky but Doc ain't playing and nobody else says shit. It's quiet like when Doc's shooting. Quiet as death and Sky don't know what to do. Can't wipe that lame look off his face and can't back off and can't hand the pill to Doc neither. He just stands there with his arm stretched out and his rusty fingers wrapped round the ball. Can't hold it much longer, can't let it go.

Seems like I coulda strolled over to Doc's stoop for a drinka water and strolled back and those two still be standing there. Doc and Sky. Billy Moon off to one side so it's just Doc and Sky.

Everybody holding they breath. Everybody want it over with and finally Doc says, Forget it, Sky. Just don't play with my shots anymore. And then Doc say, Who has next winners?

If Doc was joking nobody took it for no joke. His voice still hard. Doc ain't kidding around.

Who's next? I want to run.

Now Doc knows who's next. Leroy got next winners and Doc knows Leroy always saves a spot so he can pick up a big man from the losers. Leroy tell you to your face, I got my five, man, but everybody know Leroy saving a place so he can build him a winner and stay on the court. Leroy's a cold dude that way, been that way since he first started coming round and ain't never gon change and Doc knows that, everybody knows that but even Leroy ain't cold enough to say no to Doc. I got it, Doc.

You got your five yet?

You know you got a spot with me, Doc. Always did. Then I'ma run.

Say to myself, Shit … Good God Almighty. Great Googa-Mooga. What is happening here? Doc can't see shit. Doc blind as this bench I'm sitting on. What Doc gon do out there?

Well, it ain't my game. If it was, I'd a lied and said I had five. Or maybe not. Don't know what I'da done, to tell the truth. But Leroy didn't have no choice. Doc caught him good. Course Doc knew all that before he asked.

Did Doc play? What kinda question is that? What you think I been talking about all this time, man? Course he played. Why the fuck he be asking for winners less he was gon play? Helluva run as I remember. Overtime and shit. Don't re-member who won. Somebody did, sure nuff. Leroy had him a strong unit. You know how he is. And Doc? Doc ain't been out on the court for a while but Doc is Doc, you know. Held his own …

If he had tried to tell her about Doc, would it have made a difference? Would the idea of a blind man playing basketball get her attention or would she have listened the way she lis-tened when he told her stories he'd read about slavery days

when Africans could fly, change themselves to cats and hum-
mingbirds, when black hoodoo priests and conjure queens
were feared by powerful whites even though ordinary black
lives weren't worth a penny. To her it was folklore, supersti-
tion. Interesting because it revealed the psychology, the
pathology of the oppressed. She listened intently, not because she thought she'd hear truth. For her, belief in magic
was like belief in God. Nice work if you could get it. Her
skepticism, her hardheaded practicality, like the smallness of
her hands, appealed to him. Opposites attracting. But more
and more as the years went by, he'd wanted her with him,
wanted them to be together . . .

They were walking in Regent Park. It was clear to both of
them that things weren't going to work out. He'd never seen
her so beautiful, perfect.

There should have been stars. Stars at least, and perhaps a
sickle moon. Instead the edge of the world was on fire. They
were walking in Regent Park and dusk had turned the tree
trunks black. Beyond them in the distance, below the fading
blue of sky, the colors of sunset were pinched into a narrow,
radiant band. Perhaps he had listened too long. Perhaps he
had listened too intently for his own voice to fill the emptiness. When he turned back to her, his eyes were glazed,
stinging. Grit, chemicals, whatever it was coloring, poison-
ing the sky, blurred his vision. Before he could blink her into
focus, before he could speak, she was gone.

If he'd known Doc's story he would have said: *There's still a chance. There's always a chance. I mean this guy, Doc. Christ. He was stone blind. But he got out on the court and played. Over there. Right over there. On that very court across the hollow from us. It happened I've talked to people about it many times. If Doc could do that, then anything's possible. We're possible …*

*If a blind man could play basketball, surely we …* If he had known Doc's story, would it have saved them? He hears himself saying the words. The ball arches from Doc's fingertips, the miracle of it sinking. Would she have believed any of it?

# Hunger

## Anzia Yezierska

Shenah Pessah paused in the midst of scrubbing the stairs of the tenement. "Ach!" she sighed. "How can his face still burn so in me when he is so long gone? How the deadness in me flames up with life at the thought of him!"

The dark hallway seemed flooded with white radiance. She closed her eyes that she might see more vividly the beloved features. The glowing smile that healed all ills of life and changed her from the weary drudge into the vibrant creature of joy.

It was all a miracle — his coming, this young professor from one of the big colleges. He had rented a room in the very house where she was janitress so as to be near the people he was writing about. But more wonderful than all was the way he stopped to talk to her, to question her about herself as though she were his equal. What warm friendliness had prompted him to take her out of her dark basement to the library where there were books to read!

And then—that unforgettable night on the way home, when the air was poignant with spring! Only a moment—a kiss—a pressure of hands! And the world shone with light—the empty, unlived years filled with love!

She was lost in dreams of her one hour of romance when a woman elbowed her way through the dim passage, leaving behind her the smell of herring and onions.

Shenah Pessah gripped the scrubbing-brush with suppressed fury. "Meshugeneh! Did you not swear to yourself that you would tear his memory out from your heart? If he would have been only a man I could have forgotten him. But he was not a man! He was God Himself! On whatever I look shines his face!"

The white radiance again suffused her. The brush dropped from her hand. "He—he is the beating in my heart! He is the life in me—the hope in me—the breath of prayer in me! If not for him in me, then what am I? Deadness—emptiness—nothingness! You are going out of your head. You are living only on rainbows. He is no more real—

"What is real? These rags I wear? This pail? This black hole? Or him and the dreams of him?" She flung her challenge to the murky darkness.

"Shenah Pessah! A black year on you!" came the answer from the cellar below. It was the voice of her uncle, Moisheh Rifkin.

"Oi weh!" she shrugged young shoulders, wearied by joyless toil. "He's beginning with his hollering already." And she hurried down.

"You piece of earth! Worms should eat you! How long does it take you to wash up the stairs? " he stormed. "Yesterday, the eating was burned to coal; and to-day you forget the salt."

"What a fuss over a little less salt!"

"In the Talmud it stands a man has a right to divorce his wife for only forgetting him the salt in his soup."

"Maybe that's why Aunt Gittel went to the grave before her time—worrying how to please your taste in the mouth."

The old man's yellow, shriveled face stared up at her out of the gloom. "What has he from life? Only his pleasure in eating and going to the synagogue. How long will he live yet?" And moved by a surge of pity, "Why can't I be a little kind to him?"

"Did you chop me some herring and onions?" he interrupted harshly.

She flushed with conscious guilt. Again she wondered why ugly things and ugly smells so sickened her.

"What don't you forget?" His voice hammered upon her ears. "No care lays in your head. You're only dreaming in the air."

Her compassion was swept away in a wave of revolt that left her trembling. "I can't no more stand it from you! Get yourself somebody else!" She was surprised at her sudden spirit.

"You big mouth, you! That's your thanks for saving you from hunger."

"Two years already I'm working the nails off my fingers and you did n't give me a cent."

"Beggerin! Money yet, you want? The minute you get enough to eat you turn up your head with freshness. Are you used to anything from home? What were you out there in Savel? The dirt under people's feet. You're already forgetting how you came off from the ship—a bundle of rags full of holes. If you lived in Russia a hundred years would you have lived to wear a pair of new shoes on your feet?"

"Other girls come naked and with nothing to America and they work themselves up. Everybody gets wages in America—"

"Americanerin! Did n't I spend out enough money on your ship-ticket to have a little use from you? A thunder should strike you!"

Shenah Pessah's eyes flamed. Her broken fingernails pierced the callous flesh of her hands. So this was the end—the awakening of her dreams of America! Her memory went back to the time her ship-ticket came. In her simple faith she had really believed that they wanted her—her father's brother and his wife who had come to the new world before ever she was born. She thought they wanted to give her a chance for happiness, for life and love. And then she came—to find the paralytic aunt—housework—janitor's drudgery. Even after her aunt's death, she had gone on uncomplainingly, till her uncle's nagging had worn down her last shred of self-control.

"It's the last time you'll holler on me!" she cried. "You'll never see my face again if I got to go begging in the street." Seizing her shawl, she rushed out. "Woe is me! Bitter is me! For what is my life? Why did n't the ship go under and drown me before I came to America?"

Through the streets, like a maddened thing, she raced, not knowing where she was going, not caring. "For what should I keep on suffering? Who needs me? Who wants me? I got no-body—nobody!"

And then the vision of the face she worshiped flashed be-fore her. His beautiful kindness that had once warmed her into new life breathed over her again. "Why did he ever come but to lift me out of my darkness into his light?"

Instinctively her eyes sought the rift of blue above the ten-ement roofs and were caught by a boldly printed placard: "HANDS WANTED." It was as though the sign swung open on its hinges like a door and arms stretched out inviting her to enter. From the sign she looked to her own hands—vig-orous, young hands—made strong through toil.

Hope leaped within her. "Maybe I got yet luck to have it good in this world. Ach! God from the *sky*! I'm so burning to live—to work myself up for a somebody! And why not?" With clenched fist she smote her bosom. "Ain't everything possible in the new world? Why is America but to give me the chance to lift up my head with everybody alike?"

Her feet scarcely touched the steps as she ran up. But when she reached the huge, iron door of Cohen Brothers, a terror seized her. "Oi weh! They'll give a look on my greenhorn rags, and down I go—For what are you afraid, you fool?" she commanded herself. "You come not to beg. They need hands. Don't the sign say so? And you got good, strong hands that can turn over the earth with their strength. America is before you. You'll begin to earn money. You'll dress yourself up like a person and men will fall on their knees to make love to you—even him—himself!"

All fear had left her. She flung open the door and beheld the wonder of a factory—people—people—seas of bent heads and busy hands of people—the whirr of machinery—flying belts—the clicking clatter of whirling wheels—all seemed to blend and fuse into one surging song of hope—of new life—a new world—America!

A man, his arms heaped with a bundle of shirts, paused at sight of the radiant face. Her ruddy cheeks, the film of innocence shining out of eyes that knew no guile, carried him back to the green fields and open plains of his native Russia.

"Her mother's milk is still fresh on her lips," he murmured, as his gaze enveloped her.

The bundle slipped and fell to her feet. Their eyes met in spontaneous recognition of common race. With an embarrassed laugh they stooped to gather up the shirts.

"I seen downstairs hands wanted," came in a faltering voice.

"Then you're looking for work?" he questioned with keen interest. She was so different from the others he had known in his five years in this country. He was seized with curiosity to know more

"You ain't been long in America?" His tone was an unconscious caress.

"Two years already," she confessed. "But I ain't so green like I look," she added quickly, overcome by the old anxiety.

"Trust yourself on me," Sam Arkin assured her. "I'm a feller that knows himself on a person first off. I'll take you to the office myself. Wait only till I put away these things."

Grinning with eagerness, he returned and together they sought the foreman.

"Good luck to you! I hope you'll be pushed up soon to my floor," Sam Arkin encouraged, as he hurried back to his machine.

Because of the rush of work and the scarcity of help, Shenah Pessah was hired without delay. Atremble with excitement, she tiptoed after the foreman as he led the way into the workroom.

"Here, Sadie Kranz, is another learner for you." He addressed a big-bosomed girl, the most skillful worker in the place.

"Another greenhorn with a wooden head!" she whispered to her neighbor as Shenah Pessah removed her shawl. "Gevalt! All these greenhorn hands tear the bread from our mouths by begging to work so cheap."

But the dumb appeal of the immigrant stirred vague memories in Sadie Kranz. As she watched her run her first seam, she marveled at her speed. " I got to give it to you, you have a quick head." There was conscious condescension in her praise.

Shenah Pessah lifted a beaming face. "How kind it was from you to learn me! You good heart!"

No one had ever before called Sadie Kranz "good heart." The words lingered pleasantly. "Ut! I like to help anybody, so long it don't cost me nothing. I get paid by the week anyhow," she half apologized.

Shenah Pessah was so thrilled with the novelty of the work, the excitement of mastering the intricacies of her machine, that she did not realize that the day was passed until the bell rang, the machines came to a halt, and the "hands" made a wild rush for the cloak-room.

"Oi weh! Is it a fire?" Shenah Pessah blanched with dread.

Loud laughter quelled her fears. "Greenie! It's six o'clock. Time to go home," chorused the voices.

"Home?" The cry broke from her. "Where will I go? I got no home." She stood bewildered, in the fast-dwindling crowd of workers. Each jostling by her had a place to go. Of them all, she alone was friendless, shelterless!

"Help me find a place to sleep! " she implored, seizing Sadie Kranz by the sleeve of her velvet coat. "I got no people. I ran away."

Sadie Kranz narrowed her eyes at the girl. A feeling of pity crept over her at sight of the outstretched, hungry hands.

"I'll fix you by me for the while." And taking the shawl off the shelf, she tossed it to the forlorn bundle of rags. "Come along. You must be starved for some eating."

As Shenah Pessah entered the dingy hallroom which Sadie

Kranz called home, its chill and squalor carried her back to the janitor's basement she had left that morning. In silence she watched her companion prepare the hot dogs and potatoes on the oil-stove atop the trunk. Such pressing sadness weighed upon her that she turned from even the smell of food.

"My heart pulls me so to go back to my uncle." She swallowed hard her crust of black bread. "He's so used to have me help him. What'll he do—alone?"

"You got to look out for yourself in this world." Sadie Kranz gesticulated with a hot potato. "With your quickness, you got a chance to make money and buy clothes. You can go to shows—dances. And who knows—maybe meet a man to get married."

"Married? You know how it burns in every girl to get herself married—that's how it burns in me to work myself up for a person."

"Ut! For what need you to work yourself up. Better marry yourself up to a rich feller and you're fixed for life."

"But him I want—he ain't just a man. He is—" She paused seeking for words and a mist of longing softened the heavy peasant features. "He is, the golden hills on the sky. I'm as far from him as the earth is from the stars."

"Yok! Why wills itself in you the stars?" her companion ridiculed between swallows.

Shenah Pessah flung out her hands with Jewish fervor. "Can I help it what's in my heart? It always longs in me for the higher. Maybe he has long ago forgotten me, but only one hope drives in me like madness—to make myself alike to him."

"I'll tell you the truth," laughed Sadie Kranz, fishing in the pot for the last frankfurter. "You are a little out of your head—plain mehsugeh."

"Mehsugeh?" Shenah Pessah rose to her feet vibrant with new resolve. "Mehsugeh?" she challenged, her peasant youth afire with ambition. "I'll yet show the world what's in me. I'll not go back to my uncle—till it rings with my name in America."

She entered the factory, the next day, with a light in her face, a sureness in her step that made all pause in wonder. "Look only! How high she holds herself her head! Has the matchmaker promised her a man?"

Then came her first real triumph. Shenah Pessah was raised above old hands who had been in the shop for years and made assistant to Sam Arkin, the man who had welcomed her that first day in the factory. As she was shown to the bench beside him, she waited expectantly for a word of welcome. None came. Instead, he bent the closer to his machine and the hand that held the shirt trembled as though he were cold, though the hot color flooded his face.

Resolutely, she turned to her work. She would show him how skillful she had become in those few weeks. The seams sped under her lightning touch when a sudden clatter startled her. She jumped up terror-stricken.

"The belt! The belt slipped! But it's nothing, little bird,"

Sam Arkin hastened to assure her. "I'll fix it." And then the quick warning, "Sh-h! The foreman is coming!"

Accustomed to her uncle's harsh bickering, this man's gentleness overwhelmed her. There was something she longed to say that trembled on her lips, but her voice refused to come.

Sam Arkin, too, was inarticulate. He felt he must talk to her, must know more of her. Timidly he touched her sleeve. "Lunch-time—here—wait for me," he whispered, as the foreman approached.

A shrill whistle—the switch thrown—the slowing-down of the machines, then the deafening hush proclaiming noon. Followed the scraping of chairs, raucous voices, laughter, and the rush on the line to reach the steaming cauldron. One by one, as their cups of tea were filled, the hungry workers dispersed into groups. Seated on window-sills, table-tops, machines, and bales of shirts, they munched black bread and herring and sipped tea from saucers. And over all rioted the acrid odor of garlic and onions.

Rebecca Feist, the belle of the shop, pulled up the sleeve of her Georgette waist and glanced down at her fifty-nine-cent silk stocking. "A lot it pays for a girl to kill herself to dress stylish. Give only a look on Sam Arkin, how stuck he is on that new hand."

There followed a chorus of voices. "Such freshness! We been in the shop so long and she just gives a come-in and grabs the cream as if it's coming to her."

"It's her innocent looking baby eyes that fools him in—"

"Innocent! Pfui! These make-believe innocent girls! Leave it to them! They know how to shine themselves up to a feller!"

Bleemah Levine, a stoop-shouldered, old hand, grown gray with the grayness of unrelieved drudgery, cast a furtive look in the direction of the couple. "Ach! The little bit of luck! Not looks, not smartness, but only luck, and the world falls to your feet." Her lips tightened with envy. "It's her green-horn, red cheeks—"

Rebecca Feist glanced at herself in the mirror of her vanity bag. It was a pretty, young face, but pale and thin from undernourishment. Adroitly applying a lip-stick, she cried indignantly: "I wish I could be such a false thing like her. But only, I'm too natural—the hypocrite! "

Sadie Kranz rose to her friend's defense. "What are you falling on her like a pack of wild dogs, just because Sam Arkin gives a smile on her? He ain't marrying her yet, is he?"

"We don't say nothing against her," retorted Rebecca Feist, tapping her diamond-buckled foot, "only, she pushes herself too much. Give her a finger and she'll grab your whole hand. Is there a limit to the pushings of such a green animal? Only a while ago, she was a learner, a nobody, and soon she'll jump over all our heads and make herself for a forelady.

Sam Arkin, seated beside Shenah Pessah on the window-sill, had forgotten that it was lunchhour and that he was savagely hungry. "It shines so from your eyes," he beamed.

"What happy thoughts lay in your head?"

"Ach! When I give myself a look around on all the people laughing and talking, it makes me so happy I'm one of them."

"Ut! These Americanerins! Their heads is only on ice-cream soda and style."

"But it makes me feel so grand to be with all these hands alike. It's as if I just got out from the choking prison into the open air of my own people."

She paused for breath—a host of memories overpowering her. "I can't give it out in words," she went on. "But just as there ain't no bottom to being poor, there ain't no bottom to being lonely. Before, everything I done was alone, by myself. My heart hurt so with hunger for people. But here, in the factory, I feel I'm with everybody together. Just the sight of people lifts me on wings in the air."

Opening her bag of lunch which had lain unheeded in her lap, she turned to him with a queer, little laugh, "I don't know why I'm so talking myself out to you—"

"Only talk more. I want to know everything about yourself." An aching tenderness rushed out of his heart to her, and in his grave simplicity he told her how he had overheard one of the girls say that she, Shenah Pessah, looked like a "greeneh yenteh," just landed from the ship, so that he cried out, "Gottuniu! If only the doves from the sky were as beautiful!"

They looked at each other solemnly—the girl's lips parted, her eyes wide and serious. "That first day I came to the shop, the minute I gave a look on you, I felt right away, here's somebody from home. I used to tremble so to talk to a man, but you— you—I could talk myself out to you like thinking in myself."

"You're all soft silk and fine velvet," he breathed reverently. "In this hard world, how could such fineness be?"

An embarrassed silence fell between them as she knotted and unknotted her colored kerchief.

"I'll take you home? Yes?" he found voice at last.

Under lowered lashes she smiled her consent.

"I'll wait for you downstairs, closing time." And he was gone.

The noon hour was not yet over, but Shenah Pessah returned to her machine. "Shall I tell him?" she mused. "Sam Arkin understands so much, shall I tell him of this man that burns in me? If I could only give out to some one about him in my heart—it would make me a little clear in the head." She glanced at Sam Arkin furtively. "He's kind, but could he understand? I only made a fool from myself trying to tell Sadie Kranz." All at once she began to sob without reason. She ran to the cloak-room and hid from prying eyes, behind the shawls and wraps. The emptiness of all for which she struggled pressed upon her like a dead weight, dragging her down, down—the reaction of her ecstasy.

As the gong sounded, she made a desperate effort to pull herself together and returned to her work.

The six o'clock whistles still reverberated when Sam Arkin hurried down the factory stairs and out to the corner where he was to meet Shenah Pessah. He cleared his throat to greet her as she came, but all he managed was a bashful grin. She was so near, so real, and he had so much to say—if he only knew how to begin.

He cracked his knuckles and bit his fingertips, but no words came. "Ach! You yok! Why ain't you saying something?" He wrestled with his shyness in vain. The tense silence remained unbroken till they reached her house.

"I'm sorry"—Shenah Pessah colored apologetically—"But I got no place to invite you. My room is hardly big enough for a push-in of one person."

"What say you to a bite of eating with me?" he blurted.

She thought of her scant supper upstairs and would have responded eagerly, but glancing down at her clothes, she hesitated. "Could I go dressed like this in a restaurant?"

"You look grander plain, like you are, than those twisted up with style. I'll take you to the swellest restaurant on Grand Street and be proud with you!"

She flushed with pleasure. "Nu, come on, then. It's good to have a friend that knows himself on what's in you and not what's on you, but still, when I go to a place, I like to be dressed like a person so I can feel like a person."

"You'll yet live to wear diamonds that will shine up the street when you pass!" he cried.

Through streets growing black with swarming crowds of toil-released workers they made their way. Sam Arkin's thick hand rested with a lightness new to him upon the little arm tucked under his. The haggling pushcart peddlers, the newsboys screaming, "Tageblatt, Abendblatt, Herold," the roaring noises of the elevated trains resounded the paean of joy swelling his heart.

"America was good to me, but I never guessed how good till now." The words were out before he knew it. "Tell me only, what pulled you to this country?"

"What pulls anybody here? The hope for the better. People who got it good in the old world don't hunger for the new."

A mist filled her eyes at memory of her native village. "How I suffered in Savel. I never had enough to eat. I never had shoes on my feet. I had to go barefoot even in the freezing winter. But still I love it. I was born there. I love the houses and the straw roofs, the mud streets, the cows, the chickens and the goats. My heart always hurts me for what is no more."

The brilliant lights of Levy's Café brought her back to Grand Street.

"Here is it." He led her in and over to a corner table. "Chopped herring and onions for two," he ordered with a flourish.

"Ain't there some American eating on the card?" interposed Shenah Pessah.

He laughed indulgently. "If I lived in America for a hundred years I could n't get used to the American eating. What can make the mouth so water like the taste and the smell from herring and onions?"

"There's something in me—I can't help—that so quickly takes on to the American taste. It's as if my outside skin only was Russian; the heart in me is for everything of the new world—even the eating."

"Nu, I got nothing to complain against America. I don't like the American eating, but I like the American dollar. Look only on me!"

He expanded his chest. "I came to America a ragged nothing—and—see—" He exhibited a bank book in four figures, gesticulating grandly, "And I learned in America how to sign my name!"

"Did it come hard to learn?" she asked under her breath.

"Hard?" His face purpled with excitement. "It would be easier for me to lift up this whole house on my shoulders than to make one little dot of a letter. When I took my pencil—Oi weh! The sweat would break out on my face! 'I can't, I can't!' I cried, but something in me jumped up. 'You can— you yok—you must!'—Six months, night after night, I stuck to it and I learned to twist around the little black hooks till it means—me—Sam Arkin."

He had the rough-hewn features of the common people, but he lifted his head with the pride of a king. "Since I can write out my name, I feel I can do anything. I can sign checks, put money in the bank, or take it out without nobody to help me."

As Shenah Pessah listened, unconsciously she compared Sam Arkin, glowing with the frank conceit of the self-made man, his neglected teeth, thick, red lips, with that of the Other One—made ever more beautiful with longings and dreams.

"But in all these black years, I was always hoping to get to the golden country," Sam Arkin's voice went on, but she heard it as from afar. "Before my eyes was always the shine of the high wages and the easy money and I kept pushing myself from one city to another, and saving and saving till I saved up enough for my ship-ticket to the new world. And then when I landed here, I fell into the hands of a cockroach boss."

"A cockroach boss?" she questioned absently and reproached herself for her inattention. "A black year on him! He was a landsman, that's how he fooled me in. He used to come to the ship with a smiling face of welcome to all the greenhorns what had nobody to go to. And then he'd put them to work in his sweatshop and sweat them into their grave."

"Don't I know it?" she cried with quickened understanding. "Just like my uncle, Moisheh Rifkin."

"The blood-sucker!" he gasped. "When I think how I slaved for him sixteen hours a day—for what? Nothing!"

She gently stroked his hand as one might a child in pain. He looked up and smiled gratefully.

"I want to forget what's already over. I got enough money now to start for myself—maybe a tailor-shop—and soon—I—I want to marry myself—but none of those crazy chickens for me." And he seemed to draw her unto himself by the intensity of his gaze.

Growing bolder, he exclaimed: "I got a grand idea. It's Monday and the bank is open yet till nine o'clock. I'll write over my bankbook on your name? Yes?"

"My name?" She fell back, dumbstruck.

"Yes—you—everything I only got—you—" he mumbled. "I'll give you dove's milk to drink—silks and diamonds to wear—you'll hold all my money."

She was shaken by this supreme proof of his devotion.

"But I—I can't—I got to work myself up for a person. I got a head. I got ideas. I can catch on to the Americans quicker'n lightning."

"My money can buy you everything. I'll buy you teachers. I'll buy you a piano. I'll make you for a lady. Right away you can stop from work." He leaned toward her, his eyes welling with tears of earnestness.

"Take your hard-earned money? Could I be such a beggerin?"

"God from the world! You are dearer to me than the eyes from my head! I'd give the blood from under my nails for you! I want only to work for you—to live for you—to die for you—" He was spent with the surge of his emotion.

Ach! To be loved as Sam Arkin loved! She covered her eyes, but it only pressed upon her the more. Home, husband, babies, a breadgiver for life!

And the Other—a dream—a madness that burns you up alive. "You might as well want to marry yourself to the President of America as to want him. But I can't help it. *Him and him only* I want."

She looked up again. "No—no!" she cried, cruel in the self-absorption of youth and ambition. "You can't make me for a person. It's not only that I got to go up higher, but I got to push myself up by myself, by my own strength—"

"Nu, nu," he sobbed. "I'll not bother you with me—only give you my everything. My bank-book is more than my flesh and blood—only take it, to do what you want with it."

Her eyes deepened with humility. "I know your goodness—but there's something like a wall around me—him in my heart."

"Him?" The word hurled itself at him like a bomb-shell. He went white with pain. And even she, immersed in her own thoughts, lowered her head before the dumb suffering on his face. She felt she owed it to him to tell him.

"I wanted to talk myself out to you about him yet before.—He ain't just a man. He is all that I want to be and am not yet. He is the hunger of me for the life that ain't just eating and sleeping and slaving for bread."

She pushed back her chair and rose abruptly. "I can't be inside walls when I talk of him. I need the earth, the whole free sky to breathe when I think of him. Come out in the air."

They walked for a time before either spoke. Sam Arkin followed where she led through the crooked labyrinth of streets. The sight of the young mothers with their nursing infants pressed to their bared bosoms stabbed anew his hurt. Shenah Pessah, blind to all but the vision that obsessed her, talked on. "All that my mother and father and my mother's mother and father ever wanted to be is in him. This fire in me, it's not just the hunger of a woman for a man—it's the hunger of all my people back of me, from all ages, for light, for the life higher!"

A veil of silence fell between them. She felt almost as if it were a sacrilege to have spoken of that which was so deeply centered within her.

Sam Arkin's face became lifeless as clay. Bowed like an old man, he dragged his leaden feet after him. The world was dead—cold—meaningless. Bank-book, money—of what use were they now? All his years of saving could n't win her. He was suffocated in emptiness.

On they walked till they reached a deserted spot in the park. So spent was he by his sorrow that he lost the sense of time or place or that she was near.

Leaning against a tree, he stood, dumb, motionless, unutterable bewilderment in his sunken eyes.

"I lived over the hunger for bread—but this—" He clutched at his aching bosom.

"Highest One, help me!" With his face to the ground he sank, prostrate.

"Sam Arkin!" She bent over him tenderly. "I feel the emptiness of words—but I got to get it out. All that you suffer I have suffered, and must yet go on suffering. I see no end. But only—there is a something—a hope—a help out—it lifts me on top of my hungry body—the hunger to make from myself a person that can't be crushed by nothing nor nobody—the life higher!"

Slowly, he rose to his feet, drawn from his weakness by the spell of her. "With one hand you throw me down and with the other you lift me up to life again. Say to me only again, your words," he pleaded, helplessly.

"Sam Arkin! Give yourself your own strength!" She shook him roughly. "I got no pity on you, no more than I got pity on me."

He saw her eyes fill with light as though she were seeing something far beyond them both. "This," she breathed, "is only the beginning of the hunger that will make from you a person who'll yet ring in America."

# The Barber's Unhappiness

## George Saunders

1.

Mornings the barber left his stylists inside and sat out front of his shop, drinking coffee and ogling every woman in sight. He ogled old women and pregnant women and women whose photographs were passing on the sides of buses and, this morning, a woman with close-cropped black hair and tear-stained cheeks, who wouldn't be half bad if she'd just make an effort, clean up her face a little and invest in some decent clothes, some white tights and a short skirts maybe, knee boots and a cowboy hat and a cigarillo, say, and he pictured her kneeling on a crude Mexican sofa, in a little mud hut, daring him to take her, and soon they'd screwed their way into some sort of beanfield while some gaucho guys played soft guitars, although actually he'd better put the gaucho guys behind some trees or a rock wall so they wouldn't get all hot and bothered from watching the screwing and swoop down and stab him and have their way with Miss Hacienda as he bled to death, and come to think of it, forget the gauchos altogether, he'd just put some soft guitars on the stereo in the hut and leave the door open, although actually what was a stereo doing in a Mexican hut? Were there outlets? Plus how could he meet her? He could compliment her hair, then ask her out for coffee. He could say that as a hair-care professional, he knew a little about hair, and boy did she ever have great hair, and by the way did she like coffee? Except they always said no. Lately no no no was all he got. Plus he had zero access to a beanfield or a mud hut. They could do it in his yard but it wouldn't be the same because Jeepers had basically made of it a museum of poop, plus Ma would call 911 at the first hint of a sexy moan.

Now those, those on that meter maid, those were some serious hooters. Although her face was sort of beat. But if you could take those hooters and slap them on Miss Hacienda, wow, then you'd be talking. Just the meter maid's hooters and some decent clothes and a lip wax and the super sexy voice of the librarian who looked away whenever he ogled her, and you'd have his perfect woman, and wow would they ever be happy together forever, as long as she kept a positive attitude, which come to think of it might be an issue, because why the heck was she crying in public?

Miss Hacienda passed through a gap in a hedge and disappeared into the Episcopal church.

Why was she going to church on a weekday? Maybe she had a problem. Maybe she was knocked up. Maybe if he followed her into the church and told her he knew a little about problems, having been born with no toes, she'd have coffee with him. He was tired of going home to just Ma. Lately she'd been falling asleep with her head on his shoulder while they watched TV. Sometimes he worried that somebody would look in the window and wonder why he'd married such an old lady. Plus sometimes he worried that Ma would wake up and catch him watching the black girl in the silver bikini riding her horse through that tidal pool in slow motion on 1–900–DREMGAL.

He wondered how Miss Hacienda would look in a silver bikini in slow motion. Although if she was knocked up she shouldn't be riding a horse. She should be sitting down, taking it easy. Somebody should be bringing her a cup of tea. She should move in with him and Ma. He wouldn't rub it in that she was knocked up. He'd be loving about it. He'd be a good friend to her and wouldn't even try to screw her, and pretty soon she'd start wondering why not and start really wanting him. He'd be her labor coach and cheerfully change diapers in the wee hours and finally when she'd lost all the weight she'd come to his bed and screw his brains out in gratitude, after which he'd have a meditative smoke by the window and decide to marry her. He nearly got tears in his eyes thinking of how she'd get tears in her eyes as he went down on one knee to pop the question, a nice touch the dolt who'd knocked her up wouldn't have thought of in a million years, the nimrod, and that SOB could drive by as often as he wanted, deeply regretting his foolishness as the baby frolicked in the yard, it was too late, they were a family, and nothing would ever break them up.

But he'd have to remember to stick a towel under the door while meditatively smoking or Ma would have a cow, because after he smoked she always claimed everything smelled like smoke, and make him wash every piece of clothing in the house. And they'd better screw quietly if they weren't married, because Ma was old-fashioned. It was sort of a pain living with Ma. But Miss Hacienda had better be prepared to tolerate Ma, who was actually pretty good company when she stayed on her meds, and so what if she was nearly eighty and went around the house flossing in her bra? It was her damn house. He'd better never hear Miss Hacienda say a word against Ma, who'd paid his way through barber college, like for example asking why Ma had thick sprays of gray hair growing out of her ears, because that would kill Ma, who was always reminding the gas man she'd been a dish in high school. How would Miss Hacienda like it if after a lifetime of hard work she got wrinkled and forget-ful and some knocked-up slut dressed like a Mexican cowgirl moved in and started complaining about her ear hair? Who did Miss Hacienda think she was, the Queen of Sheba? She could go into labor in the damn Episcopal church for all he cared, he'd keep wanking it in the pantry on the little milking stool for the rest of his life before he'd let Ma be hurt, and that was final.

As Miss Hacienda came out of the church she saw a thick-waisted, beak-nosed, middle-aged man rise angrily from a wooden bench and stomp into Mickey's Hairport, slamming the door behind him.

2.

Next morning Ma wanted an omelet. When he said he was running late she said never mind in a tone that made it clear she was going to accidentally/on purpose burn herself again while ostensibly making her own omelet. So he made the omelet. When he asked was it good, she said it was fine, which meant it was bad and he had to make pancakes. So he made pancakes. Then he kissed her cheek and flew out the door, very very late for Driving School.

Driving School was being held in what had been a trendy office park in the Carter years and was now a flat white overgrown stucco bunker with tinted windows and a towable signboard that said: *Driving School*. Inside was a conference table that filled most of a room that smelled like a conference table sitting in direct sunlight with some spilled burned coffee on it.

"Latecomers will be beaten," said the Driving School instructor.

"Sorry," said the barber.

"Joking!" said the instructor, thrusting a disorderly wad of handouts at the barber, who was trying to get his clipons off. "What I was just saying was that, our aim is, we're going to be looking at some things or aspects, in terms of driving? Meaning safety, meaning, is speeding something we do in a vacuum, or could it involve a pedestrian or fatality or a family out for a fun drive, and then here you come, speeding, with the safety or destiny of that family not held firmly in your mind, and what happens next? Who knows?"

"A crash?" said someone.

"An accident?" said someone else.

"Crash or accident both could," said the instructor. "Either one might or may. Because I've seen, in my CPR role as a paramedic, when many times, and I'm sorry if you find this gross or too much, I've had to sit in our rescue vehicle with a cut-off arm or hand, even of a kid, a really small arm or even a limb, just weeping as if I hadn't been thoroughly trained, as I know none of you have, but I have, and why was I holding that small arm or limb and bawling? Because of someone like you yourselves, good people, I know you are, I'm not saying that, but you decided what? What did you decide? Or they. That person who cut off that kid's arm I was carrying that day I was just saying?"

No one knew.

"They decided to speed is what you did," said the instructor sadly, with pity for both the armless child and the otherwise good people who on that fateful day had decided to speed, and now sat before him, lives ruined.

"I didn't his nobody," said a girl in a T-shirt that said *Buggin'*. "Cop just stopped me."

"But I'm talking the possibility aspect?" the instructor said kindly. "I'm talking what happens if you walk away from here a man or a woman not changed in her thought patterns by the material I'm about to present you in terms of the visuals and graphics? Which some of the things are crashes and some are working wounds I myself have personally dressed and some are wounds we downloaded off the Internet so you could have a chance to see wounds that are national? Because why? Because consequences. Because are we on this earth or an island?"

"Oh," said the Buggin' girl, who now seemed chastened and convinced.

Outside the tinted window were a little forest and a stream and an insurance agency and a FedEx drop-off tilted by some pipeline digging. There were six students. One was the barber. One was a country boy with a briefcase, who took laborious notes and kept asking questions with a furrowed brow, as if, having been caught speeding, he was now considering a career in law enforcement. Did radar work via sonar beams? How snotty did someone have to get before you could stun them with your stun gun? Next to the country boy was the Buggin' girl. Next to the Buggin' girl was a very very happy crew-cut older man in a cowboy shirt and bolo tie who laughed at everything and seemed to consider it a great privilege to be here at the Driving School on this particular day with this particular bunch of excellent people, and who by the end of the session had proposed holding a monthly barbecue at his place so they wouldn't lose touch. Across the table from the Happy Man was a white-haired woman about the barber's age, who kept making sly references to films and books the barber had never heard of a rolling her eyes at things the instructor said, while writing *Help Me!* and *Beam Me UP!* on her notepad and shoving it across the table for the Happy Man to read, which seemed to make the Happy Man uncomfortable.

Next to the white-haired woman was a pretty girl. A very pretty girl. Wow. One of the prettiest girls the barber had ever seen. Boy was she pretty. Her hair was crimped and waist-length and her eyes were doelike and Egyptian and about her there was a sincerity and intelligence that made it hard for him to look away. She certainly looked out of place here at the conference table, with one hand before her in a strip of sunlight that shone on a very pretty turquoise ring that seemed to confirm her as someone exotic and darkish and schooled in things Eastern, someone you could easily imagine making love to on a barge on the Nile, say, surrounded by thousands of candles that smelled weird, or come to think of it, maybe she was American Indian, and he saw her standing at the door of a tipi wearing that same sincere and intelligent expression as he came home from the hunt with a long string of dead rabbits, having been accepted into the tribe at her request after killing a cute white rabbit publicly to prove he was a man of the woods, or actually they had let him skip the rabbit part because he had spoken to them so frankly about the white man's deviousness and given them secret information about an important fort after first making them promise not to kill any more women or children. He pictured one of the braves saying to her, as she rubbed two corncobs together in the dying sunlight near a spectacular mesa, that she was lucky to have the barber, who had powerful medicine in terms of being a powerful medicine man, and silently she smiled, rubbing the corncobs together perhaps a little faster, remembering the barber naked in their tipi, although on closer inspection it appeared she was actually probably Italian.

The girl looked up and caught him staring at her. He dropped his eyes and began leafing through his course materials.

After a number of slides of terrible wounds, the instructor asked did anyone know how many g's a person pulled when he or she went through a windshield at eighty miles per after hitting a bridge abutment or a cow. No one knew. The instructor said quite a few. The Happy Man said he'd had a feeling it was quite a few, which was why, wasn't it, that people died? The instructor said either that or flying debris or having one's torso absolutely crushed.

"I guess that would do it," said the Happy man, grinning.

"So what's my point?" the instructor said, pointing with his pointer to an overhead of a cartoon man driving a little car toward a tombstone while talking gaily on a car phone. "Say we're feeling good, very good, or bad, which is the opposite, say we've just had a death or a premonition or the birth of a child or a fight with our wife or spouse, but my point is, we're experiencing an emotional peak? Because what we then maybe forget, whether happy or fighting or sad or glad, whatever, is that two tons of car is what, is the thing you are in, inside of, driving, and I hope not speeding or otherwise, although for the sake of this pretend example I'm afraid we have to assume yes, you are, which is how this next bad graphic occurs."

Now on the overhead the cartoon man's body parts were scattered and his car phone was flying up to heaven on little angel wings. The barber looked at the pretty girl again. She smiled at him. His heart began to race. This never happened. They never smiled back. Well, she was young. Maybe she did-n't know better than to smile back at an older guy you did-n't want. Or maybe she wanted him. It was possible. Maybe she'd had it with young horny guys just out for a few quick rolls in the hay. Maybe she wanted someone old enough to really appreciate her, who didn't come too quickly and owned his own business and knew how to pick up after himself. He hoped she was a very strict religious virgin who'd never even had a roll in the hay. Not that he hoped she was frigid. He hoped she was the kind of strict religious virgin who, once married, would let it all hang out, and when not letting it all hang out would move with quiet dignity in conservative clothes so that no one would suspect how completely and to-

tally she could let it all hang out when she chose to, and that
she came from a poor family and could therefore really appreciate the hard work that went into running a small business, and maybe even had some accounting experience and
could help with the books. Although truthfully, even if she'd
had hundreds of rolls in the hay and couldn't add a stinking
row of figures, he didn't care, she was so pretty, they'd work
it out, assuming of course she'd have him, and with a sinking
heart he remembered his missing toes. He remembered that
day at the lake with Mary Ellen Kovksi, when it had been
over a hundred and he'd sat on a beach chair fully dressed,
claiming to be chilly. A crowd of Mary Ellen's friends had
gathered to help her undress him and throw him in, and in
desperation he'd whispered to her about his toes, and she'd
gone white and called off her friends and two months later
married Phil Anpesto, that idiotic beanpole. Oh, he was tired
of hiding his toes. He wanted to be open about them. He
wanted to be loved in spite of them. Maybe this girl had a
wisdom beyond her years. Maybe her father had a deformity,
a glass eye, or facial scar, maybe through long years of loving
this kindly but deformed man she had come to almost need
the man she loved to be somewhat deformed. Not that he
liked the idea of her trotting after a bunch of deformed guys,
and also not that he considered himself deformed, exactly,
although, admittedly, ten barely discernable bright-pink nubs
were no picnic. He pictured her lying nude in front of a fireplace, so comfortable with his feet that she'd given each nub

a pet name, and maybe sometimes during lovemaking she got a little carried away and tried to kiss or lick his nubs, although certainly he didn't expect that, and in fact found it sort of disgusting, and for a split second thought somewhat less of her, then pictured himself gently pulling her up, away from his feet, and the slightly shamed look on her face made him forgive her completely for the disgusting thing she'd been about to do out of her deep deep love for him.

The instructor held up a small bloodied baby doll, which he then tossed across the room into a trunk.

"Blammo," he said. "Let's let that trunk represent a crypt or a tomb, and it's our fault, from speeding, how then do you feel?"

"Bad," said the Buggin' girl.

The pretty girl passed the barber the Attendance Log, which had to be signed to obtain Course Credit and Associated Conviction Waivers/Point Reductions.

They looked frankly at each other for what felt like a very long time.

"Hokay!" the instructor said brightly. "I suppose I don't have to grind you into absolute putty, so now it's a break, so you don't view me as some sort of Marquis de Sade or harsh taskmaster requiring you to watch gross visuals and graphics until your mind rots out."

The barber took a deep breath. He would speak to her. Maybe buy her a soda. The girl stood up. The barber got a shock. Her face was the same lovely exotic intelligent slim

Cleopatran face, but her body seemed scaled to a head twice the size of the one she had. She was a big girl. Her arms were round and thick. Her mannerisms were a big girl's mannerisms. She hunched her shoulders and tugged at her smock. He felt a little miffed at her for having misled him and a little miffed at himself for having ogled such a fatty. Well, not a fatty, exactly, her body was okay, it seemed solid enough, it was just too big for her head. If you could somehow reduce the body to put it in scale with the head, or enlarge the head and shrink down the entire package, then you'd have a body that would do justice to that beautiful beautiful face, that, even now, tidying up his handouts, he was regretting having lost.

"Hi," she said.

"Hello," he said, and went outside and sat in his car, and when she came out with two Cokes pretended to be cleaning the ashtrays until she went away.

3.

Later that month the barber sat stiffly at a wedding reception at the edge of a kind of mock Japanese tearoom at the Hilton while some goofball inside a full-body Puppet-Players groom costume, complete with top hat and tails and a huge yellow felt head and three-fingered yellow felt hands, made vulgar thrusting motions with his hips in the barber's direction, as if to say: Do you like to do this? Have you done this? Can you show me how to do this, because soon I'm going to have to do this with that PuppetPlayers bride over there who is right now flirting—hey!—flirting with that bass player! and the PuppetPlayers groom sprinted across the dance floor and began romping pugilistically around the bass player who'd been trying to cuckold him. Everyone was laughing and giving the barber inexplicable thumbs-up as the PuppetPlayers groom dragged the PuppetPlayers bride across the dance floor and introduced her to the barber, and she appeared to be very taken with him, and sat on his lap and forced his head into her yellow felt cleavage, which was stained with wine and had a big cigarette burn at the neckline. With many gestures she bade the barber look under her skirts, and overcome with embarrassment he did so, eventually finding a wrapped box which, when opened, revealed a wrapped cylinder which, when opened, shot a banner across the dance floor, and on the banner was written: BEST O' LUCK ARNIE AND EVELYN FROM MOM AND POP. The PuppetPlayers newlyweds sprinted across the room and bowed low before Arnie and Evelyn, who were sitting sullenly on the bandstand, apparently in the middle of a snit.

"Mickey!" Uncle Edgar shouted to the barber. "Mickey, you should've boffed that puppet broad! So what if she's a puppet! You're no prize! You're going to be choosy? Think of it! Think of it! Arnie's half your age!"

"Edgar for Christ's sake you're embarrassing him!" shouted Aunt Jean. "It's like you're saying he's old! It's like you're saying he's an old maid, only he's a guy! See what I mean? You think that's nice?"

"I am!" shouted Uncle Edgar, "I am saying that! He's a damned old lady! I don't mean no offense! I'm just saying to get out and live! I love him! That's why I'm saying! The sun's setting! Pork some young babe, and if you like it, if you like the way she porks, what the hell, put down roots! What do you care? Love you can learn! But you gotta start somewhere! I mean my God, even these little so-and-sos here are trying to get some of it!"

And Uncle Edgar threw a dinner roll at a bunch of adolescent boys the barber vaguely remembered having once pulled around the block in a little red wagon. The boys gave Uncle Edgar the finger and confirmed that not only were they trying to get some of it, they were actually getting some of it, and not always from the same chick, and sometimes more than once a day, and sometimes right after football practice, and quite possibly in the near future from a very hot Shop teacher they had reason to believe would probably give it to all of them at once if only they approached it the right way.

"Holy cow!" shouted Uncle Edgar. "Let me go to that school!"

"Edgar, you pig, be logical!" shouted Aunt Jean. "Just because Mickey's not married don't mean he ain't getting any! He could be getting some from a lady friend, or several lady friends, lady friends his own age, who already know the score, whose kids are full-grown! You don't know what goes on in his bed at night!"

"At least I don't think he's queer!" Uncle Edgar shouted to the adolescents the barber now remembered having loaded sleeping into a minivan on the evening of the day, years before, when he'd pulled them in the red wagon.

"If he is we don't give a rat's ass," said one of the adolescents. "That's his business."

"We learned that in school," said another. "Who You Do Is Up To You. We had a mini-session."

Now the PuppetPlayers groom was trying to remove the real bride's garter, and some little suited boys were walking a ledge along a goldfish stream that separated the Wedding Area from the Okinawa Memories, where several clearly non-Japanese women in kimonos hustled drinks, sounding a huge metal gong whenever anyone ordered a double, at which time a bartender dressed like a sumo sent a plastic sparrow across the room on a guy wire. The little suited boys began prying up the screen that kept the goldfish from going over a tiny waterfall, to see if they would die in a shallow pond near the Vending Area.

"For example those kids torturing those fish," shouted Uncle Edgar. "You know who those kids are? Them are Brendan's kids. You know who Brendan is? He's Dick's kid. You remember who Dick is? Your second cousin the same age as you, man! Remember I took you guys to the ballgame and he threw up in my Rambler? So them kids are Dick's grandkids and here Dick's the same age as you, which means you're old enough to be a grandpa, grandpa, but you ain't even a pa yet, which I don't know how you feel about it but I think is sort of sad or weird!"

"You do but maybe he don't!" shouted Aunt Jean. "Why do you think everything you think is everything everybody else thinks? Plus Dick's no saint and neither are those kids. Dick was a teen dad and Brendan was a teen dad and probably those kids on that ledge are going to be teen dads as soon as they finish killing those poor fish!"

"Agreed!" shouted Uncle Edgar. "Hey, I got no abiding love for Dick. You want to have a fight with me at a wedding over my feelings for Dick, who throwing up in my Rambler was just the start of the crap he's pulled on me? All's I'm saying is, there's no danger of Mickey here being a teen dad, and he better think about what I'm saying and get on the stick before his shooter ain't a viable shooter anymore!"

"I'm sure you start talking about the poor guy's shooter at a wedding!" shouted Aunt Jean. "You're drunk!"

"Who ain't?" shouted Uncle Edgar and the table exploded in laughter and one of the adolescents fell mock-drunk off his chair and when this got a laugh all the other adolescents fell mock-drunk off their chairs.

The barber excused himself and walked quickly out of the Wedding Area past three stunning girls in low-cut white gowns, who stood in what would have been shade from the fake overhanging Japanese cherry trees had the trees been outside and had it been daytime.

In the bathroom the Oriental theme receded and all was shiny chrome. The barber peed, mentally defending himself against Uncle Edgar. First off, he'd had plenty of women.

Five. Five wasn't bad. Five was more than most guys, and for sure it was more than Uncle Edgar, who'd married Jean right out of high school and had a lower lip like a fish. Who would Uncle Edgar have had him marry? Sara DelBianco, with her little red face? Ellen Wiest, that tall drink of water? Ann De-Mann, who was swaybacked and had claimed he was a bad screw? Why in the world was he, a successful small business-man, expected to take advice from someone who'd spent the best years of his life transferring partial flanges from one conveyor belt to another while spraying them with a protec-tive solvent mist? Uncle Edgar could take a flying leap, that drunk, why didn't he mind his own beeswax and spray him-self with a protective solvent mist and leave the ambitious entrepreneurs of the world alone, the lush?

The barber wet his comb the way he'd been wetting his comb since high school and prepared to slick back his hair. A big vital man with a sweaty face came in and whacked the barber on the back as if they were old pals. In the mirror was a skeletal mask of blue and purple and pink that the barber knew was his face but couldn't quite believe was his face, because in the past his face had always risen to the oc-casion. In the past his face could always be counted on to amount to more than the sum of its parts when he smiled winningly, but now when he smiled winningly he looked like a corpse trying to appear cheerful in a wind tunnel. His eyes bulged, his lips were thin, his forehead wrinkles were deep as sticklines in mud. It had to be the lighting. He was ugly. He was old. How had this happened? Who would want him now?

"You look like hell," thundered the big man from a stall, and the barber fled the mirror without slicking back his hair.

As he rushed past the stunning girls, a boy in a fraternity sweatshirt came over. Seeing the barber, he made a comic geriatric coughing noise in his throat, and one of the girls giggled and adjusted her shoulder strap as if to keep the barber from seeing down her dress.


4.

A few weeks before the wedding, the barber had received in the mail a greeting card showing a cowboy roping a steer. The barber's name was scrawled across the steer's torso, and *Me, (Mr. Jenks)* across the cowboy.

*Here's hoping you will remember me from our driving school,* said a note inside, *and attend a small barbecue at my home. My hope being to renew those acquaintances we started back then, which I found enjoyable and which since the loss of my wife I've had far too few of. Please come and bring nothing. As you can see from the cover, I am roping you in, not to brand you, but only to show you my hospitality, I hope. Your friend, Larry Jenks.*

Who was Jenks? Was Jenks the Happy Man? The barber threw the card in the bathroom trash, imagining the Driving School kooks seated glumly on folding chairs in a trailer house. For a week or so the card sat there, cowboy-side up, vaguely reproaching him. Then he took out the trash.

A few days after the wedding he received a second card from Jenks, with a black flower on the front.

*A good time was had by all,* it said. *Sorry you were unable to attend. Even the younger folks, I think, enjoyed. Many folks took home quite a few sodas, because as I am alone now, I never could have drank that many sodas in my life. This note, on a sadder note, and that is why the black flower, is to inform you that Eldora Ronsen is moving to Seattle. You may remember her as the older woman to your immediate right. She is high up in her company and just got higher, which is good for her, but bad for us, as she is such a super gal. Please join us Tuesday next, Corrigan's Pub, for farewell drinks, map enclosed, your friend, Larry Jenks.*

Tuesday next was tomorrow.

"Well, you can't go," Ma said. "The girls are coming over."

The girls were the Holy Name Society. When they came over he had to wait on them hand and foot while they talked about which priest they would marry if only the priests weren't priests. When one lifted her blouse to show her recent scar, he had to say it was the worst scar ever. When one asked if her eye looked rheumy he had to get very close to her rheumy eye and say it looked non-rheumy to him.

"Well, I think I might want to go," he said.

"I just said you can't," she said. "The girls are coming."

She was trying to guilt him. Once she'd faked a seizure when he tried to go to Detroit for a hair show. No wonder he had no friends. Not that he had no friends. He had plenty of friends. He had Rick the mailman. Every day when Rick the mailman came in, he asked the barber how it was hanging, and the barber said fine, fine, it was hanging fine. He had old Mr. Mellon, at Mellon Drugs, next door to the shop who, though sort of deaf, was still a good friend, when not hacking phlegm into his little red cup.

"Ma," he said. "I'm going."

"Mr. Bigshot," she said. "Bullying an old lady."

"I'm not bullying you," he said. "And you're not old."

"Oh, I'm young, I'm a tiny baby," she said, tapping her dentures.

That night he dreamed of the pretty but heavy girl. In his dream she was all slimmed down. Her body looked like the body of Daisy Mae in the Li'l Abner cartoon. She came into the shop in cut-off jeans, chewing a blade of grass, and said she found his accomplishments amazing, especially considering the hardships he'd had to overcome, like his dad dying young and his mother being so nervous, and then she took the blade of grass out of her mouth and put it on the magazine table and stretched out across the Waiting Area couch while he undressed, and seeing his unit she said it was the biggest unit she'd ever seen, and arched her back in a sexy way, and seeing his nubs she said his feet were so special, so distinctive, they actually turned her on they were so unusual, and then she called him over and gave him a deep warm kiss on the mouth that was so much like the kiss he'd been waiting for all his life that it abruptly woke him.

Sitting up in bed, he missed her. He missed how much she loved and understood him. She knew everything about him and yet still liked him. His gut sort of ached with wanting.

In his boyhood mirror he caught sight of himself. He looked like a little old man startled from sleep. What in the world? Still sitting, he flexed his chest the way he used to flex his chest in the weightlifting days, and looked so much like a little old man trying to take a dump in his bed that he hopped up and stood panting on the round green rug.

Ma was blundering around in the hallway. Because of the dream he had a partial bone. To hide his partial bone, he kept his groin behind the door as he thrust his head into the hall.

"I was walking in my sleep," Ma said. "I'm so worried I was walking in my sleep."

"What are you worried about?" he said.

"I'm worried about when the girls come," she said.

"Well, don't worry," he said. "It'll be fine."

"Thanks a million," she said, going back into her room. "Very reassuring."

Well, it would be fine. What could happen? If they ran out of coffee, one of the old ladies could make coffee, if they ran out of snacks they could go a little hungry, if something really disastrous happened they could call him at Corrigan's, he'd leave Ma the number.

Because he was going.

In the morning he called Jenks and accepted the invitation, while Ma winced and clutched her stomach and pulled over a heavy wooden chair and collapsed into it.

5.

Corrigan's was meant to feel like a pub at the edge of a Scottish golf course, there was a roaring fire, and many ancient-looking golf clubs hanging above tremendous tables of a hard plastic material meant to appear gnarled and scarred, and kilted waitresses with names like Heather and Zoe were sloshing chicken wings and fried cheese and lobster chunks into metal vats near an aerial photo of the Old Course at St. Andrew's, Scotland.

The barber was early. He liked to be early. He felt it was polite to be early, except when he was late, at which time he felt being early was anal and being late was sort of dashing. But today he was early. Where the heck was everybody? They weren't very polite. This was dumb. He didn't even know if the pretty but heavy girl was coming. Plus how heavy was she anyway? He couldn't exactly remember. He looked down at his special shoes. They were blocky and black, and had big removable metal stays in the sides and squeaked when he walked. Well if anybody said anything about his shoes they could go to hell, he hadn't asked to be born with no toes, and besides, the special shoes looked nice with khakis.

"Sorry we're late!" Mr. Jenks shouted, and the Driving School group settled in around the long gnarled table.

The pretty but heavy girl hung her purse across the back of her chair. Her hair looked like her hair in the dream and her eyes looked like her eyes in the dream, and as for her body, he couldn't tell, she was wearing a muumuu. But certainly facially she was pretty. Facially she was very possibly the prettiest girl here. Was she? The facially prettiest? If aliens came down and forced each man to pick one woman to reproduce with in a chain-link enclosure while they took notes, would he choose her, based solely on face? Here was a woman with a good rear but a doglike face, here was a woman with a nice perm but a blop at the end of her nose, here was the Buggin' girl, who looked like a chicken, here was the white-haired woman, whose face was all wrinkled, here was the pretty but heavy girl. Was she the prettiest? Facially? He thought she very possibly was.

He regarded her fondly from across the table, waiting for her to catch him regarding her fondly, so he could quickly avert his eyes, so she'd know he was still possibly interested, and then she dropped her menu and bent to retrieve it and the barber had a chance to look briefly down her dress.

Well she definitely had something going on in the chest category. So facially she was the prettiest in the room, plus she had decent boobs. Attractive breasts. The thing was, would she want him? He was old. Oldish. When he stood up too fast his knee joints popped. Lately his gums had started to bleed.

Plus he had no toes. Although why sell himself short? He owned his own small business. He had a bit of a gut, yes, and his hair was somewhat thin, but then again his shoulders and chest were broad, so that the overall effect, even with the gut, was of power, which girls liked, and at least his head was properly sized for his body, which was more than she could say, although then again he still lived with his mother.

Well, who was perfect? He wasn't perfect and she wasn't perfect but they obviously had some sort of special chemistry, based on what had happened at the Driving School, and anyway, what the heck, he wasn't proposing, he was just considering possibly trying to get to know her somewhat better.

In this way he decided to ask the pretty but heavy girl out.

On the big-screen TV a woman in a white dress stood on a porch. A dinosaur came up the driveway and the woman appeared to be chewing him out because he was late. The dinosaur slunk away, head down, but returned a few seconds later with a tremendous bouquet of roses, a bouquet the size of a phone booth, which he then dropped on the woman, whose legs were shown protruding lifelessly from under the bouquet.

How to do it, that was the thing. How to ask her. He could get her alone and say her hair looked super. While saying it looked super he could run a curl through his fingers in a professional way, as if looking for split ends. He could say he'd love a chance to cut such excellent hair, then slip her a card for One Free Cut and Coffee. That could work. That had worked in the past. It had worked with Sylvia Reynolds, a bank teller with crow's-feet and a weird laugh who turned out to be an excellent kisser. When she'd come in for her Free Cut and Coffee, he'd claimed they were out of coffee, and had taken her to Bean Men Roasters. A few dates later they'd gotten carried away, unfortunately, because of her excellent kissing, and done more, much more actually, than he ever would've imagined doing with someone with crow's-feet and a weird laugh and strangely wide hips, and when he'd gotten home that night and had a good hard look at the locket she'd given him after they'd done it, he'd instantly felt bad, because wow could you ever see the crow's-feet in that picture. As he looked at Sylvia standing in that bright sunlit meadow in the picture, her head thrown back, joyfully laughing, her crow's-feet so very pronounced, a spontaneous image had sprung into his mind of her coming wide-hipped toward him while holding a baby, and suddenly he'd been deeply disappointed in himself for doing it with someone so unusual-looking, and to ensure that he didn't make matters worse by inadvertently doing it with her a second time, he'd sort of never called her again, and had even switched banks.

He glanced at the pretty but heavy girl and found her making her way toward the Ladies'.

Now was as good a time as any.

He waited a few minutes, then excused himself and stood outside the Ladies' reading ads posted on a corkboard. A man was looking for a chain saw and a boy or man to run it.

A woman had hit a deer and did anyone want to buy some possibly risky venison? An innovative method of reading was available, in which one read every other line, and this version of the method had proven far superior to the previous version of the method, which in some cases caused severe eye strain.

The pretty but heavy girl came out.

He cleared his throat and asked was she having fun?

She said yes.

Then he said wow did her hair look great. And in terms of great hair, he knew what he was talking about, he was a professional. Where did she have it cut? He ran one of her curls through his fingers, as if looking for split ends, and said he'd love the chance to work with such dynamite hair, and took from his shirt pocket the card for One Free Cut and Coffee.

"Maybe you could stop by sometime," he said.

"That's nice of you," she said, and blushed.

So she was a shy girl. Sort of cutely nerdy. Not exactly confident. That was too bad. He liked confidence. He found it sexy. On the other hand, who could blame her, he could sometimes be very intimidating. Also her lack of confidence indicated he could perhaps afford to be a little bit bold.

"Like, say, tomorrow?" he said. "Like, say, tomorrow at noon?"

"Ha," she said. "You move quick."

"Not too quick, I hope," he said.

"No," she said. "Not too quick."

So her had her. By saying he wasn't moving too quick, wasn't she implicitly implying that he was moving at exactly the right speed? All he had to do now was close the deal.

"I'll be honest," he said. "I've been thinking about you since Driving School."

"You have?" she said.

"I have," he said, and it was basically true.

"So you're saying tomorrow?" she said, blushing again.

"If that's okay for you," he said.

"It's okay for me," she said.

Then she started uncertainly back to the table and the barber raced into the Men's. Yes! Yes, yes, yes. It was a date. He had her. He couldn't believe it. He'd really played that smart. What had he been worried about? He was cute, women had always considered him cute, never mind the thin hair and minor gut, there was just something about him women liked.

Wow she was pretty, he had done very well for himself.

Back at the table Mr. Jenks was taking Polaroids. He announced his intention of taking six shots of the Driving School group, one for each member to keep, and the barber stood behind the pretty but heavy girl, with his hands on her shoulders, and at one point she reached up and gave his wrist a little squeeze.

6.

At home old-lady cars were in the driveway and old-lady coats were piled on the couch and the house smelled like old lady and the members of the Altar and Rosary Society were gathered around the dining room table looking frail. They all looked the same to the barber, he could never keep them straight, there was a crone in a lime pantsuit and a crone in a pink pantsuit and two crones in blue pantsuits. As he came in they began asking Ma where he had been, why was he out so late, why hadn't he been here to help, wasn't he normally a fairly good son? And Ma said yes, he was normally a fairly good son, except he hadn't given her any grandkids yet and often wasted water by bathing twice a day.

"My son had that problem," said one of the blue crones. "His wife once pulled me aside."

"Has his wife ever pulled you aside?" the pink crone said to Ma.

"He's not married," said Ma.

"Maybe the not-married is related to the bathing-too-often," said the lime crone.

"Maybe he holds himself aloof from others," said the blue crone. "My son held himself aloof from others."

"My daughter holds herself aloof from others," said the pink crone.

"Does she bathe too often?" said Ma.

"She doesn't bathe too often," said the pink crone. "She just thinks she's smarter than everyone."

"Do you think you're smarter than everyone?" asked the lime crone severely, and thank God at that moment Ma reached up and pulled him down by the shirt and roughly kissed his cheek.

"Have a good time?" she said, and the group photo fell out of his pocket and into the dip.

"Very nice," he said.

"Who are these people?" she said, wiping a bit of dip off the photo with her finger. "Are these the people you went to meet? Who is this you're embracing? This big one."

"I'm not embracing her, Ma," he said. "I'm just standing behind her. She's a friend."

"She's big," Ma said. "You smell like beer."

"Did you girls see Mrs. Link last Sunday?" said the lime crone. "Mrs. Link should never wear slacks. When she wears slacks her hips look wide. Her hips are all you see."

"They almost seem to precede her into the church," said the pink crone.

"It's as if she is being accompanied by her own hips," said the lime crone.

"Some men like them big," said one of the blue crones.

"Look at his face," said the other blue crone. "He likes them big."

"The cat who ate the canary," said the lime crone.

"Actually, I don't consider her big," said the barber, in a tone of disinterested interest, looking down over the pink crone's shoulder at the photo.

"Whatever you say," said the lime crone.

"He's been drinking," said Ma.

Oh he didn't care what they thought, he was happy. He jokingly snatched the photo away and dashed up to his room, taking two stairs at a time. These poor old farts, they were all superlonely, which was why they were so damn mean.

Gabby Gabby Gabby, her name was Gabby, short for Gabrielle.

Tomorrow they had a date for lunch.

Breakfast, rather. They'd moved it up to breakfast. While they'd been kissing against her car she said she wasn't sure she could wait until lunch to see him again. He felt the same way. Even breakfast seemed a long time to wait. He wished she were sitting next to him on the bed right now, holding his hand, listening through the tiny vined window to the sounds of the crones cackling as they left. In his mind he stroked her hair and said he was glad he'd finally found her, and she said she was glad to have been found, she'd never dreamed that someone so distinguished, with such a broad chest and wide shoulders, could love a girl like her. Was she happy? He tenderly asked. Oh she was so happy, she said, so happy to be sitting next to this accomplished, distinguished man in this amazing house, which in his mind was not the current house, a pea-green ranch with a tilted cracked sidewalk, but a mansion, on a lake, with a smaller house nearby for Ma, down a very very long wooded path, and he'd paid cash for the mansion with money he'd made from his international chain of barbershops, each of which was an exact copy of his current barbershop, and when he and Gabby visited his London England shop, leaving Ma behind in the little house, his English barbers would always burst into applause and say Jolly Good Jolly Good as the happy couple walked in the door.

"I'm leaving you the dishes, Romeo," Ma shouted from the bottom of the stairs.

7.

Early next morning he sat in the bath, getting ready for his date. Here was his floating weinie, like some kind of sea creature, here were his nubs on the tile wall. He danced them nervously around a bit, like Fred Astaire dancing on a wall, and swirled the washrag through the water, holding it by one corner, so that it too was like a sea creature, a blue ray, a blue monogrammed ray that now crossed the land that was his belly and attacked the sea creature that was his weinie, and remembering what Uncle Edgar had said at the wedding about his shooter not being viable, he gave his shooter a good, hard, reassuring shake, as if congratulating it for being so very viable. It was a great shooter, very good, perfectly fine, in spite of what Ann DeMann had once said about him being a bad screw, it had gotten hard quick last night and stayed hard throughout the kissing, and as far as being queer, that was laughable, he wished Uncle Edgar could have seen that big boner.

Oh he felt good, in spite of a slight hangover he was very happy.

Flipping his unit carelessly from side to side with thumb and forefinger, he looked at the group Polaroid, which he'd placed near the sink. God, she was pretty. He was so lucky. He had a date with a pretty young girl. Those crones were nuts, she wasn't big, no bigger than any other girl. Not much bigger anyway. How wide were her shoulders compared to, say, the shoulders of the Buggin' girl? Well, he wasn't going to dignify that with a response. She was perfect just the way she was. He leaned out of the tub to look closer at the photo. Well, Gabby's shoulders were maybe a little wider than the Buggin' girl's shoulders. Definitely wider. Were they wider than the shoulders of the white-haired woman? Actually in the photo they were even wider than the shoulders of the country boy.

Oh, he didn't care, he just really liked her. He liked her laugh and the way she had of raising one eyebrow when skeptical, he liked the way that, when he move his hand to her boob as they leaned against her car, she let out a happy little sigh. He liked how, after a few minutes of kissing her while feeling her boobs, which were super, very firm, when he dropped his hand down between her legs, she said she thought that was probably enough for one night, which was good, it showed good morals, it showed she knew when to call it quits.

Ma was in her room, banging things around.

Because for a while there last night he'd been worried. Worried she wasn't going to stop him. Which would have been disappointing. Because she barely knew him. He could've been anybody. For a few minutes there against the car he'd wondered if she wasn't a little on the easy side. He wondered this now. Did he? Did he wonder this now? Did he want to wonder this now? Wasn't that sort of doubting her? Wasn't that sort of disloyal? No, no it was fine, there was no sin in looking at things honestly. So was she? Too easy? In other words, why so sort of desperate? Why had she so quickly agreed to go out with him? Why so willing to give it away so easily to some old guy she barely knew? Some old balding guy she barely knew? Well, he thought he might know why. Possibly it was due to her size. Possibly the guys her own age had passed her by, due to the big bod, and nearing thirty, she'd heard her biologic clock ticking and decided it was time to lower her standards, which, possibly, was where he came in. Possibly, seeing him at the Driving School, she'd thought: Since all old guys like young girls, big bods notwithstanding, this old pear-shaped balding guy can ergo be had no problem.

Was that it? Was that how it was?

Did he want to be thinking this?

"Some girl just called," Ma said, leaning heavily against the bathroom door. "Some girl, Gabby or Tabby or something? Said you had a date. Wanted you to know she's running late. Is that the same girl? The same fat girl you were embracing?"

Sitting in the tub, he noticed that his penis was gripped nervously in his fist, and let it go, and it fell to one side, as if it had just passed out.

"Do the girl a favor, Mickey," Ma said. "Call it off. She's too big for you. You'll never stick with her. You never stick with anyone. You couldn't even stick with Ellen Wiest, for crying out loud, who was so wonderful, you honestly think you're going to stick with this Tabby or Zippy or whatever?"

Of course Ma had to bring up Ellen Wiest. Ma had loved Ellen, who had a regal face and great manners and was always kissing up to Ma by saying what a great mother Ma was. He remembered the time he and Ellen had hiked up to Butternut falls and stood getting wet in the mist, holding hands, smiling sweetly at each other, which had really been fun, and she'd said she thought she loved him, which was nice, except wow she was tall. You could only hold hands with her for so long before your back started to hurt. He remembered his back sort of hurting in the mist. Plus they'd had that fight on the way down. Well, there were a lot of things about Ellen that Ma wasn't aware of, such as her nasty temper, and he remembered Ellen storming ahead of him on the trail, glaring back now and then, just because he'd made a funny remark about her height, about her blocking out the sun, and hadn't he also said something about her being able to eat leaves from the tallest of the trees they were passing under? Well, that had been funny, it had all been in fun, why did she have to get so mad about it? Where was Ellen now? Hadn't she married Ed Trott? Well, Trott could have her. Trott was probably suffering the consequences of being married to Miss Thin Skin even now, and he remembered having recently seen Ed and Ellen at the ValueWay, Ellen pregnant and looking so odd, with her big belly pressing against the cart as she craned that giraffelike neck down to nuzzle Ed, who had a big stupid happy grin on his face like he was the luckiest guy in the world.

The barber stood up angrily from the tub. Here in the mirror were his age-spotted deltoids, and his age-spotted roundish pecs and his strange pale love handles.

Ma resettled against the door with a big whump.

"So what's the conclusion, lover boy?" she said. "Are you canceling? Are you calling up and canceling?"

"No I'm not," he said.

"Well, poor her," Ma said.

8.

Every morning of his life he'd walked out between Ma's twin rose trellises. When he went to grade school, when he went to junior high, when he went to high school, when he went to barber college, he'd always walked out between the twin trellises. He walked out between them now, in his brown cords and blue button-down, and considered plucking a rose for Gabby, although that was pretty corny, he might seem sort of doddering, and instead, using the hand with which he'd been about to pluck the rose, he flicked the rose, then in his mind apologized to the rose for ripping its skin.

Oh, this whole thing made him tense, very tense, he wished he was back in bed .

"Mickey, a word," Ma called out from the door, but he only waved to her over his shoulder.

South Street was an old wagon road. Cars took the bend too fast. Often he scowled at the speeding cars on his way to work, imagining the drivers laughing to themselves about the way he walked. Because on days when his special shoes hurt he sort of minced. They hurt today. He shouldn't have worn the thin gray socks. He was mincing a bit but trying not to, because what if Gabby drove up South on her way to meet him at the shop and saw him mincing?

On Fullerton there were three consecutive houses with swing sets. Under each swing was a grassless place. At the last of the three houses a baby sat in the grassless place, smacking a swing with a spoon. He turned up Lincoln Ave, and passed the Liquor Mart, which smelled like liquor, and Le Belle Époque, the antique store with the joyful dog inside, and as always the joyful dog sprang over the white settee and threw itself against the glass, and then there was Gabby, down the block, peering into his locked shop, and he corrected his mincing and began walking normally though it killed.

Did she like the shop? He took big bold steps with his head thrown back so he'd look happy. Happy and strong, with all his toes. With all his toes, in the prime of his life. Did she notice how neat the shop was? How professional? Or did she notice that four of his chairs were of one type and the fifth was totally different? Did it seem to her that the shop was geared to old blue-hairs, which was something he'd once heard a young woman say as he took out the trash?

How did she look? Did she look good?

It was still too far to tell.

Now she saw. Now she saw him. Her face brightened, she waved like a little girl. Oh, she was pretty. It was as if he'd known her forever. She looked so hopeful. But oops. Oh my God she was big. She'd dressed all wrong, tight jeans and a tight shirt. As if testing him. Jesus, this was the biggest he'd ever seen her look. What was she doing, testing him? Testing him by trying to look her worst? Here was an alley, should he swerve into the alley? Swerve into the alley and call her later? Or not? Not call her later? Forget the whole thing? Pretend last night had never happened? Although now she'd seen him. And he didn't want to forget the whole thing. Last night for the first time in a long time he'd felt like someone other than a guy who wanks it on the milking stool in his mother's pantry. Last night he'd bought a pitcher for the Driving School group and Jenks had called him a sport. Last night she'd said he was a sexy kisser.

Thinking about forgetting last night gave him a pit in his stomach. Forgetting last night was not an option. What were the options? Well, she could trim down. That was an option. That was a good option. Maybe all she needed was someone to tell her the simple truth, someone to sit her down and say: Look, you have an incredibly beautiful, intelligent face, but from the neck down, sweetie, wow, we've got some serious work to do. And after their frank talk, she'd send him flowers with a card that said *Thanks for your honesty, let's get this thing done.* And every night as she stood at the mirror in her panties and bra he'd point out places that needed improvement, and the next day she'd energetically address those areas in the gym, and soon the head-bod discrepancy would be eliminated, and he imagined her in a fancy dress at a little table on a veranda, a veranda by the sea, thanking him for their honeymoon trip, she came from a poor family and had never even been on a vacation, much less a six-week tour of Europe, and then she said, Honey, why not put down that boring report on how much your international chain of barbershops earned us this month and join me in the bedroom so I can show you how grateful I am, and in the bedroom she started stripping, and was good at it, not that she'd ever done it before, no, she hadn't, she was just naturally good at it, and when she was done, there she was, with her perfect face and the Daisy Mae body, smiling at him with unconditional love.

It wouldn't be easy. It would take hard work. He knew a little about hard work, having made a barbershop out of a former pet store. Tearing out a counter he'd found a dead mouse. From a sump pump he'd pulled three hardened snakes. But he'd never quit. Because he was a worker. He wasn't afraid of hard work. Was she a worker? He didn't know. He'd have to find out.

They'd find out together.

She stood behind his wooden bench, under his shop awning, and the shadow of her wild mane fell at his feet.

What a wild ride this had been, how much he had learned about himself already!

"Here I am," she said, with a shy, pretty smile.

"I'm so glad you are," he said, and bent to unlock the door of his shop.

# Frightening Love

## Yasunari Kawabata

He had loved his wife intensely. In other words, he had loved this one woman too much. He considered his wife's early death to be a punishment from heaven for his love. This was the only sense he could make of her death.

After she died, he stayed far away from any kind of woman. He would not even hire a woman to care for his house. He employed men to do the cooking and cleaning. It was not that he hated all other women, but simply that any woman reminded him of his wife. For example, to him every woman smelled of fish, just as his wife had. Wondering if this feeling itself was also heaven's punishment for loving his wife too much, he resigned himself to a life without a trace of a woman.

But there lived in his house one woman he could do nothing about. He had a daughter. And, of course, she looked more like his late wife than any woman in the world.

The girl began to attend middle school.

Once, when the light came on in the girl's room in the middle of the night, he peeped through a crack in the sliding partition. The girl was holding a small pair of scissors. Her knees were drawn up and spread apart as she used the scissors, looking down for a long time. The next day, after the girl had gone to school, he shuddered as he secretly stared at the white scissor blades.

Another night, the light in the girl's room came on again. He peeked through the crack in the partition. The girl folded a white cloth and carried it out of the room. He could hear the sound of water running. Soon the girl started a fire in the charcoal brazier. Placing the white cloth on top, she sat beside it. Then she burst into tears. When she stopped, she began to trim her nails over the cloth. The nails fell as she removed the cloth. The smell of burning nails nauseated him.

He had a dream. He dreamed that his dead wife told his daughter that he had seen her secret.

The daughter stopped looking at his face. He did not love his daughter. He shuddered when he thought that some man would be punished by heaven one day for loving this girl.

Finally, one night, a dagger in her hand, the girl eyed her father's throat. He knew it. His eyes closed in resignation. This was his punishment for loving his wife intensely, for loving one woman too much. Knowing that the girl would attack her mother's enemy, he waited for the blade.

# Permissions Acknowledgments